Sherlock Holmes and The Case of the Perplexed Politician

By

Margaret Walsh

First edition published in 2020
© Copyright 2020
Margaret Walsh

Paperback ISBN 9781787055520
ePub ISBN 978-1-78705-553-7
PDF ISBN 978-1-78705-554-4

Published by MX Publishing
335 Princess Park Manor, Royal Drive,
London, N11 3GX
www.mxpublishing.co.uk

Cover design by Brian Belanger

To John and Wendy.

Chapter One

I read in the paper this morning that Sir Algernon Leadbetter, as he became, had died in his sleep. I now feel that the time is right to set down on paper the events that began when our paths crossed with Mr. Leadbetter. Events that, even now, so many years later, fill me with horror and sadness.

It was in the early summer of 1887 that Mycroft Holmes sent Mr. Algernon Leadbetter, M.P., and his sister, Verity, to our rooms in Baker Street with a strange tale. It was a tale that would lead us into one of the most perplexing and horrifying cases we ever encountered.

I clearly remember the day the Leadbetters came to our door. It was a warm, pleasant morning, such as London gets only in summer. The day was clean and clear and full of promise.

Algernon Leadbetter was a handsome man of around thirty years old. Tall, with dark curly hair, a sharply chiselled jaw, and a high-bridged nose that, combined with keen observant eyes, gave him the look of a bird of prey. He was a member of parliament for the part of Wiltshire that nestled between Devizes and Marlborough, and a member of the Diogenes Club.

It was this last connection that had brought him to our door, upon the recommendation of Mycroft Holmes. Accompanying him was his sister, Verity, a comely lass of some twenty one years. She had hair dark that was as curly as her brother's, and the same distinguished nose, but the hawk-like eyes in her held a sweetness of disposition, rather than a fierce hunting instinct. At that moment, however, those glorious eyes held a wealth of sadness. Verity was dressed in half-mourning, whilst her brother wore a mourning band around the upper part of his right arm.

When Mr. Leadbetter had introduced himself and his sister to us, and mentioned how they came to be here, Holmes gestured to the sofa with a languid wave of his hand.

"Please, take a seat. My brother rarely wastes my time, so I can only assume that the matter that brings you here is either strange or interesting."

"It is certainly strange, Mr. Holmes, but whether you find it interesting, is an entirely different matter," said Mr. Leadbetter.

Holmes indicated with another hand wave that Mr. Leadbetter should tell us his story.

"I am perplexed, gentlemen, by an untimely death." He paused, as though uncertain as to how to continue.

Holmes murmured in an encouraging manner.

Mr. Leadbetter took a deep breath. "The part of Wiltshire that I represent is very ancient, with barrows, or burial mounds, dotting the landscape like so many giant molehills. A week ago a local lawyer, Mr. Peter Harrington, was found at the base such a barrow with a large stone resting upon him."

"An accident, surely," I said.

"That is what puzzles me, Doctor Watson," Algernon Leadbetter replied. "The rock should have crushed him, but with the rain we have had, the ground was muddy and the rock merely pushed him into the mud. The cause of death, according to the local coroner, was a fractured skull. The back of his head was crushed, but there was no sign of anything that could have caused the injury."

Holmes sat up and leaned forward, his attitude one of keen interest. "Where did the rock on top of him come from?"

"It was one of the facing stones of the barrow. I do not know if you are familiar with West Kennet Long Barrow, but this tomb is somewhat smaller version of it," Leadbetter replied. He frowned. "The barrow is on land owned by Sir Denby Hardcastle, the local squire. Harrington had no reason to be there. I could have understood it if it had been Verity." He smiled faintly at his sister. "She has been interested in the barrows since she was a child."

"So we have a man die in a place he had no business being, with a mysteriously crushed skull, and laying beneath a large rock that should have crushed him, but did not." Holmes summed up the situation. "This is indeed most interesting, Mr. Leadbetter. But why come to me? Surely this is in the purview of the Wiltshire Constabulary?"

Algernon Leadbetter looked at Holmes. "Let us just say that the police have a man dead beneath a rock and are not prepared to see anything else." He paused. "I find it a mite peculiar that a man with little interest in prehistoric monuments would end up dead at the base of one. As the man's friend, and the one who would have been his brother-in-law, I also find I have more questions than answers about the scenario." He looked at Holmes. "I do not like it, Mr. Holmes. I do not like it at all."

"What marks were there around the body?" Holmes asked.

"Marks?"

"Footprints, for example. Or marks indicating something large had been dragged, or rolled. The stone you mentioned must have go there somehow. Were there signs that it had slid down the side of the barrow? Or perhaps that it has been placed there by men?"

Algernon Leadbetter shook his head. "I do not know, Mr. Holmes. There was nothing mentioned in the police report that I saw."

"Incompetent imbeciles," Holmes muttered.

I looked at Miss Leadbetter. "My condolences upon your loss, Miss Leadbetter."

"Thank you, Doctor. Watson," she replied, twisting a black silk handkerchief in her dainty hands. "Peter Harrington and I had just become engaged. It had not been formally announced as yet."

That explained the half mourning rather than more usual full mourning. As the engagement had not been announced, Miss Leadbetter could not be seen to grieve excessively, though it was apparent that the lady was deeply unhappy.

Algernon Leadbetter continued, "There is also the fact that Harrington had a swan's feather held loosely in his hand. Why would a swan be near a barrow? There are far too many questions here for me to be comfortable accepting the word of the Wiltshire Constabulary that the death is merely an unfortunate accident."

Holmes nodded his agreement. "That is an attitude that I can most certainly understand." He looked from brother to sister and back again. "Well, Mr. Leadbetter, Miss Leadbetter, you have most certainly gained my attention. Doctor Watson and I will no doubt come down to Wiltshire in due course."

The siblings rose to their feet. Algernon Leadbetter shook both our hands. "Thank you, gentlemen. You have greatly relieved my mind on this matter. Your brother told me that you are the best chance we have of discovering what truly happened to Peter."

"I only hope, Mr. Leadbetter, that I can live up to my brother's glowing praises."

"Not only your brother's, Mr. Holmes. Robert Gascoyne-Cecil, our Prime Minister, and Marquess of Salisbury, also spoke highly of you. Indeed, it was he who suggested I speak with your brother upon the matter." Mr. Leadbetter smiled slightly. "I am sure you will not be surprised, knowing the rules of the Diogenes Club, to learn that I had never spoken with your brother before this morning."

They took their leave and I showed them to the front door, assisting Miss Leadbetter into the carriage that awaited them. Returning upstairs I found Holmes already deep in thought.

He looked up at me. "Well, Watson, what do you think?"

I took my seat, my brow creasing in thought. "It is a pretty puzzle, Holmes. As a medical man, I cannot see how the Wiltshire Constabulary came to their conclusions."

Holmes snorted derisively. "An accidental death means far less work for them than does a murder."

"So we are going to Wiltshire?" I asked.

"Eventually," Holmes replied. "I think I need to have a few words with Mycroft first. I want to know what he knows about Algernon Leadbetter and his sister."

Chapter Two

We called upon Mycroft at the Diogenes Club that very evening. It was obvious that Mycroft was expecting our visit. A decanter of brandy and three crystal glasses sat on a silver tray on a side table beside Mycroft's chair in the Stranger's Room.

"Sherlock. Doctor Watson. Do come in. Sit down." Mycroft waved us to a couple of comfortable armchairs drawn up near his. Mycroft poured brandy and handed us each a glass. I settled back into the chair, sipping slowly, and with great appreciation. The Diogenes Club had a superlative cellar.

Mycroft sipped at his own brandy briefly and set the glass down on the table. He turned to his brother. "I take it that Algernon Leadbetter came to see you?"

"He did. And a pretty tale he had to tell."

"Indeed. What did you make of it?"

"It certainly appears to have features of interest," Holmes commented.

"So you will be taking a little trip to Wiltshire, then?" Mycroft raised his eyebrows quizzically.

"It is distinctly possible." Holmes placed his own brandy down. "What do you know of the Leadbetters, Harrington, and Sir Denby Hardcastle, Mycroft?"

Mycroft sat in silence whilst he gathered his thoughts.

"Algernon Leadbetter was voted in as MP for his part of Wiltshire in the last election," he eventually said.

"Where exactly is his part of Wiltshire?" I asked.

"Between Marlborough and Devizes," Mycroft replied. "It is a rural community, mostly centred around the village of Barrow-upon-Kennet. His constituency boundaries almost reach both towns. Barrow-upon-Kennet itself is very old. It is mentioned in the Domesday Book."

Mycroft took a sip of his brandy, then placed the glass down again. "Verity is Algernon's only sibling. She acts as his hostess as he is not yet married. As for Sir Denby Hardcastle; he is the local squire. He resides in Barrow Hill Manor, which overlooks the village. The family has been there since the seventeenth century, I understand. Before that a royal hunting lodge stood upon the site. The site was gifted to Sir Denby's ancestor for services rendered by a suitably grateful monarch."

Holmes moved impatiently in his chair. It was obvious he did not consider the history of the manor germane to the matter at hand.

"Sir Denby is married to an American woman," Mycroft continued. "Lady Augusta is the daughter of a cattle rancher. She is…" Mycroft paused, as if looking for suitable words to describe the lady. After a moment his face settled into a look of bland inscrutability. "Well, if you are going to Wiltshire, you will see for yourselves. Lady Augusta Hardcastle is less a woman and more a force of nature, or so I have been told. I have never met her." Mycroft's tone was faintly relieved. "As for Harrington, I know nothing about him except for what Leadbetter has told me, which, no doubt, he has also told you."

Mycroft picked up his brandy and took a sip. "You will be going to Wiltshire?" he asked again.

Holmes frowned. "I believe so. This case interests me deeply. The business of the rock and the swan's feather. Yes, I do believe a visit to Wiltshire is advisable."

"I shall have a word with a few people, Sherlock," Mycroft said. "Just so the members of the Wiltshire Constabulary do not feel threatened, shall we say, by your presence."

Holmes got to his feet. "Thank you, Mycroft, your assistance is appreciated, as always."

I got to my feet and, after shaking Mycroft's hand, followed Holmes out the door.

It was another three days before we got word from Mycroft that everything was in place in Wiltshire. Holmes had spent the three days poring over a large scale map of Wiltshire that I procured for him from Stanfords on one of my many perambulations around the city, and smoking pipe after pipe of his particularly poisonous tobacco. The air in our rooms was noxious to a degree that even the normally tolerant Mrs. Hudson was moved to acidic comment.

The night before we left we sat quietly in our rooms having eaten what would be the last of Mrs. Hudson's excellent meals for a while. We both smoked our pipes, content to relax before we dove into another case. I think if I had known then what I know now, I would have baulked at setting out upon the morrow.

Holmes glanced at where the map lay folded on the desk. "Have you ever been to Wiltshire, Watson?"

I shook my head.

"It is an interesting county," Holmes said. "It has quite possibly the longest continual human occupation of any county in England

"No doubt an equally long history of crime," I observed.

Holmes smiled slightly at my weak sally, but otherwise did not respond.

Chapter Three

The sun was shining with the promise of a great deal of heat, when we left London for Swindon in Wiltshire. The rail system was such that we could not go directly to Marlborough. We had to go to Swindon, then transfer to a branch line down to Marlborough. This added several hours to our journey, but was still much quicker than attempting to make the trip by hired coach. Also much less painful. Some of the roads in rural Wiltshire were somewhat more rudimentary than the roads in London.

Holmes was silent for most of the trip, which was not unusual for him. I busied myself with an assortment of newspapers, and when I had run out of those, I watched the charming rural landscape slide past the windows. We passed charming farms and patches of woodland. I particularly noted the small grassy hillocks that dotted the landscape.

It was past time for luncheon by the time we reached Swindon. We managed a quick bite to eat at the hotel next to the train station, Irish stew with dumplings and reasonably strong coffee, before catching another train to Marlborough. Holmes still was not speaking. I had tried to engage him in conversation over lunch, but gave it up and had addressed myself to the food.

We were met on the platform at Marlborough Station by a tall, genial, young man, with dark brown curls, equally dark brown eyes, and an air of quiet competence. He was well dressed, but not excessively so, in the manner of a prosperous shop keeper or perhaps a law clerk.

"Mr. Holmes? Doctor Watson?" The young man looked from Holmes to myself.

"I am Sherlock Holmes, and this is my good friend Watson," my friend said, extending his hand and breaking his self-imposed silence, "And you are?"

The young man shook Holmes' hand and then reached to shake mine. "Inspector James Crawford, Wiltshire Constabulary."

Wiltshire Constabulary had the singular honour of being the first county wide police force in Britain. Prior to its establishment in 1839, all police forces had been set up as independent city forces, with many smaller settlements still making do with parish watchmen. A succession of ambitious and capable Chief Constables, including the current incumbent, Captain Robert Sterne, R.N., had made the Wiltshire Constabulary a true force to be reckoned with, and one that other counties were modelling their own police forces upon.

"I have been sent from Devizes with instructions to assist you in any way possible," said Inspector Crawford.

Holmes' eyebrows arched upwards. "Your superiors have changed their tune, have they not? I was under the impression that Mr. Harrington's death was considered an accident."

"The Chief Constable is a practical man, Mr. Holmes," the inspector replied. "When the local Member of Parliament starts making noises, and then you begin to receive messages from important people in London on the subject, it is usually a good idea to relax your stance and open your mind a little."

Holmes made a noise of approval.

"Rooms have been reserved for you at the Wight and Barrel pub in Barrow-upon-Kennet. I have a pony and trap waiting outside the station. I will see you both settled and you can tell me what you wish to see, and with whom you wish to speak."

Holmes clapped his hands together. "Capital idea. After you, Inspector."

We gathered up our luggage and followed Inspector Crawford out of the railway station to where a pony and trap waited for us patiently. The inspector and the trap's driver, assisted us to load our luggage, then we loaded ourselves, and were off, winding our way out of the picturesque little town of Marlborough, heading into the Wiltshire countryside.

As we drove along I noticed more of the small grassy hillocks that I had seen from the train dotting the landscape. Up close they seemed much larger than they did from the windows of the train. Inspector Crawford followed my gaze.

"You have not seen them before, doctor?" he asked politely.

"Indeed not," I replied. "It seems strange to see little hills sitting in the midst of fields of grazing animals or crops."

"They are not natural hills, doctor. Those are barrows. The burial chambers of our remote ancestors. Some are Anglo-Saxon, others are prehistoric. We tend to be rather proud of them around here."

"We?" I asked.

"I was born and raised in Barrow-upon-Kennet, or, rather upon the Hardcastle estate. That is why my superiors appointed me to the case." Inspector Crawford shrugged in a slightly self-deprecating manner. "I know the area, and the people, intimately."

"I am sure you will prove to be a great help to Holmes," I replied.

The man himself was sunk deep into his thoughts and did not respond. Inspector Crawford looked at him, then back at me, and raised his eyebrows in polite query.

"Holmes gets like this when facing an interesting problem. Pay him no mind. He is not deliberately being rude." I could not forebear smiling a little. "When he is deliberately being rude you will know about it. You and everyone else in the general vicinity."

Inspector Crawford laughed lightly.

I turned my attention back to the green beauty of Wiltshire.

After about an hour, we approached a small village. It seemed a prosperous little place. Cottages built of flint and stone and thatched with straw gave an appearance of antiquity to the place. The presence of a church that was clearly medieval, showed that the antiquity was not simply one of appearance.

The church, churchyard, and manse, dominated one side of a large, rectangular, village green. Cottages clustered at both of the shorter ends of the green. The road twisted away from the cottages at the further end and on towards a hill in the near distance, on which a large manor house could just be seen. I assumed that this was the residence of Sir Denby Hardcastle and his wife, the redoubtable Lady Augusta.

Directly opposite the church stood a collection of buildings. A blacksmith's, a small grocer's shop, and a large sprawling complex of buildings, that comprised the pub with its stables and associated out buildings.

The trap trotted around the green before drawing to a halt outside the pub. A brightly painted sign above the door, with a picture of a fantastical creature throwing barrels around, swung gently in the breeze.

Inspector Crawford saw me look at the sign. He smiled. "Get John Wright to tell you the story of the pub's name, when you get a chance. We are quite proud of it around here."

Holmes roused himself from his thoughts and looked around with a degree of interest. A large, dark-haired, middle-aged, man, sleeves rolled up to reveal muscular arms, and wearing a long white apron over his clothes, come out of the door.

Inspector Crawford jumped down from the trap and shook the main's hand. "Good to see you again, John. This is Mr. Sherlock Holmes and Doctor John Watson, down from London."

"Good to see you too, Jimmy." The man, John, looked at us. "They will be here about the lawyer's death?"

"We are," said Holmes, extending a hand. "Sherlock Holmes, sir."

The man shook his hand briskly. "John Wright, Mr. Holmes. Publican. I've set aside the small suite of rooms for yourself and Doctor Watson. It comprises two bedrooms and a snug sitting room that overlooks the green. My wife will provide breakfast, lunch, and dinner. All included in the price of the rooms."

"Capital! We could not ask for better, eh Watson?"

"Indeed not, Holmes." I reached out and shook hands with John Wright as well. "Inspector Crawford suggested I ask you about the pub's name."

He laughed. "The Wight and Barrel. I'm sure it appears an odd name to you."

"I admit that it does."

"There used to be a barrow here. Just a small one. Several hundred years ago when it was decided to build a pub on this site, the publican to be decided to level the barrow and use the space inside as his cellar. Well, the barrow-wight didn't like that one bit."

"Barrow-wight?" I asked.

John Wright scratched at the back of his neck. "It's a sort of ghost that haunts barrows," he said at last.

Holmes snorted.

"Anyway, the pub was built and the beer barrels stored, but then the trouble started. The innkeeper found that his barrels were getting chucked around in the cellar. Cracking and breaking, leaving his precious beers and ales to seep into the floor. He never could catch who was doing it. His wife suggested that it might be a barrel-wight, but he laughed at her."

"As well he should," commented Holmes drily.

"Then one night, after the pub had closed, he decided to sit outside the cellar door all night to catch who it was that was creeping down there to shift the barrels. He sat there all night, but no one tried to get in. He was well confident that his barrels would have come to no harm. Until he opened the door."

I found I was leaning forward, eager to hear the rest of the story.

"He opened the door and nearly fainted from shock. There was a bigger mess than ever before. The floor of the cellar was awash with beer. He nearly wept with the vexation of it all."

"What happened?" I asked.

"His wife, an intelligent lady, sent for the local wise-woman. She told the publican that the wight was unhappy at having his home reduced to such a state. She advised him to leave offerings for the wight of food and drink, and to apologize."

"Did it work?" I asked?

"It did, indeed, doctor. The publican tidied up the cellar, stood in the middle of it and apologized for not consulting the wight before levelling his home. Then he left a plate of food and a mug of beer each night for the wight. Every publican since does the same. Me grand-dad did, and me dad, and now I do the same. And as an extra apology to the wight, he changed the name of the pub from the Swan to The Wight and Barrel. Never had trouble again."

"Fascinating story," I exclaimed. "Thank you for telling it to us."

"You're welcome, Doctor Watson." John Wight turned and signaled to a sturdy lad who had come around the right hand side of the building. "Take the gentlemen's baggage upstairs, Paul."

Mr. Wright turned back to us. "Your belongings will be safe with my son. Come in and have a spot of dinner. You must be hungry after travelling from London. We dine early in the country."

"You might as well," Inspector Crawford told us. "I cannot get the key to Peter Harrington's rooms in Marlborough until tomorrow."

Holmes looked momentarily chagrined, then he shrugged, and looked at me. "What do you say to a good meal followed by a walk, my friend?"

"Sounds like an excellent plan to me, Holmes."

Holmes turned to the publican. "Lead on, Mr. Wright."

John Wright smiled, and ushered us in to the pub. His sturdy son followed behind us, bringing our luggage. The lad disappeared up a flight of stairs at the end of the taproom, and we were shown through a door next to them into a charming little dining room. Four tables were set with clean, white, linen, with polished oaken chairs drawn up to them. A large window looked out onto a vegetable garden; soft, green coloured curtains framed the view.

We sat at the table nearest the window, and I gazed out with some small pleasure at the rural beauties the garden offered.

A bustling, pink-cheeked woman, with bright blue eyes, and chestnut curls, entered the room from another door, which I supposed to be the kitchen. She introduced herself to us as Mrs. Wright.

"I have a nice bit of roast beef, with potatoes, peas, Yorkshire pudding and horse radish sauce. If that will suit you gentlemen."

"Sounds excellent, dear lady," I replied.

The food did indeed prove to be as excellent as it sounded. Both Holmes and I ate well, before we took a stroll around the village green to get our bearings.

Barrow-upon-Kennet was a typical English village. The pub we were staying in appeared to be of the same antiquity as the church across the green which, upon closer inspection, was dedicated to St. Nicholas. A weathered board outside informed us that the incumbent was a Reverend Simon Browning. From the front window of the manse, a small grey cat eyed us with some suspicion.

Having assured ourselves of the layout of the village, we returned to the pub and our rooms.

I settled into one of the comfortable looking chairs that was situated before a small fireplace and looked at Holmes, who was standing at the window staring out into the gathering dusk.

"What did you make of our host's story, Holmes?"

"Unmitigated piffle, Watson," came the sharp response. "There are no such things as ghosts. Or barrow-wights, nor any other sort of supernatural beastie."

I chuckled. I was well aware that the landlord's tale would have affronted the cool, logical mind of my friend. "Then how do you explain the disappearing food?"

Holmes sniffed, then turned and dropped into the other chair. He gave me a sharp look. "No doubt this hostelry has the most well-fed rats in the land. Given, as they are, a plate of good food and a mug of beer each day. Well-fed and no doubt slightly drunk as well."

"And the moving barrels?" I goaded.

"Tales grow in the telling, Watson, as you well know. Most likely several barrels were not stacked correctly and fell over. With each telling of the tale, no doubt the number of barrels and how much each one was moved grew, until we have a story of a mythical creature hurling barrels around with gay abandon."

I chuckled lightly and stopped teasing my friend. We sat in companionable silence until it was time to sleep.

I harboured some concerns that there would be some noise from the taproom, but the building was solidly constructed and no untoward sounds disturbed our slumbers.

Chapter Four

The next morning Holmes and I were breakfasting upon bacon and eggs, washed down with a good strong coffee, when Inspector Crawford arrived. He wished Mrs. Wright a good morning before joining us at table for coffee. He refused food, claiming he had already breakfasted.

"I have the pony and trap waiting out the front, gentlemen, whenever you are ready," he said.

Holmes took a last swallow of his coffee and set the cup down. "No time like the present, inspector."

I hastened up to our rooms to gather up both of our coats and then joined Holmes and Crawford at the front door of the pub.

It was a cool morning, with a little mist playing around the tops of the trees although the warmth of the sun was already making itself felt. We climbed into the trap and took the road out of the village and back to Marlborough.

"We have to call first at the legal practice Mr. Harrington worked at," Inspector Crawford said. "The principal of the practice, Mr. Aubrey Somerville, has the keys to Harrington's lodgings in his keeping. Harrington rented rooms from Somerville and his wife."

"What manner of man is Somerville?" I asked.

"A good man, for all that he is a lawyer," Crawford replied. Like most police officers he appeared to take a dim view of the legal profession. "He and his wife are very involved in the affairs of their parish. His wife visits the sick and the elderly, taking food, medicine, and comforts to them. Somerville keeps a keen eye on the local lads. Those that have promise he pays to have educated. Harrington was one such lad. Somerville paid for his education, and then took him on as a junior when he qualified as a lawyer."

"Then he will be the man best placed to tell us about Harrington," Holmes observed.

Conversation died away as we trotted on through the countryside. Holmes always found the country enervating, but for me, the greenness and freshness was a delight to the senses.

Marlborough looked particularly pretty this fine morning as we rode through her gently cobbled streets, finally drawing to a halt outside a sturdy Georgian building in one of the main thoroughfares. A discreet sign above the door announced we were before the premises of Somerville and Cannon, Barristers and Solicitors.

Aubrey Somerville was waiting for us in a well-kept, well-lit, office. Somerville was a short, elderly man, with receding silver hair, and an air of competence that made him seem imposing, despite his lack of inches. His sharp blue eyes held intelligence and grief in seemingly equal measure.

"A sorry business, gentlemen," were the words he greeted us with, waving us to chairs seated before a large mahogany desk. "I am, however, gratified that the police and Mr. Sherlock Holmes are taking an interest in my protégé's death. My dear wife is much bereft. Peter was like a son to us. If there is anything I may do to assist you in your endeavours."

"Some information, Mr. Somerville, if you would be so kind," said Holmes, taking one of the seats. "And then the keys to Mr. Harrington's rooms."

"Looking for clues, eh?

"Something of that nature," replied Holmes.

Inspector Crawford and I took the remaining chairs, and Mr. Somerville seated himself behind the desk. "Peter was a bright lad," Somerville said. "Son of a local butcher. The man died young leaving a widow and young Peter. It seemed wrong to let such intelligence as the lad had go to waste. He was quick-witted and sharp, a born lawyer, you might say."

"I understand that you paid for Mr. Harrington's education," said Holmes.

"I believe in a meritocracy, gentlemen. A society where those that are the best rise to the appropriate heights. In my small way I do what I can to make that a reality. By seeing that those with the intellect to make something of themselves get the chance to do so."

"A worthy ambition," I observed.

Aubrey Somerville turned a beaming smile upon me. "I am glad that you agree, doctor. At this moment another protégé of mine is at the University of London completing a medical degree. He will no doubt return here at some point. Marlborough is a growing town and as such can always use more professional men."

Somerville turned his attention back to Holmes. "Peter professed an interest in law, and he did well. He qualified at Cambridge, came back here as a junior in this practice with Mr. Elias Cannon and myself. Peter was well-liked by our clients, and was gathering a little cluster for whom he was their preferred legal representative." Somerville suddenly looked very old and very sad. "We were about to elevate Peter to partner. He was getting married to Algernon Leadbetter's sister. Leadbetter is a Member of Parliament, as I am sure you are aware. It would have been a good marriage. The time was right for Peter to move up, and for Elias to retire."

Silence reigned for a moment, then Somerville shook himself. "What is done, as they say, is done. Nothing can change it." He drew a set of keys from his pocket and handed them across to Inspector Crawford. "You will return these to me when you have finished?"

Crawford tucked the keys carefully into his pocket. "Of course, Mr. Somerville."

We rose to our feet, and departed, leaving the old man to his quiet melancholy.

We walked along the street, turning off the main thoroughfare into a street of tidy, well-presented houses of much the same period as the building housing the office of Somerville and Cannon.

Inspector Crawford knocked on the door of one of the larger houses, which was opened by a parlour maid. Crawford introduced us and the girl let us in. "The mistress knows you are coming, sirs, but regrets she is unable to meet you."

Holmes nodded briefly. "I understand that Mrs. Somerville is much distressed by the events."

"She is, sir."

"It is unlikely that we should need to disturb her. Please show us to Mr. Harrington's rooms, if you will, lass."

The girl inclined her head. "This way, gentlemen." She led the way up two flights of stairs and gestured to a door at the end of a short corridor. "Those were Mr. Peter's rooms."

Crawford took the keys from his pocket. "Thank you, Harriet. We will not keep you."

The girl, Harriet, bobbed a quick curtsey and headed back down the stairs. Crawford jangled the keys in his hand. "Shall we?"

Holmes waved at him to get on with it. Crawford inserted a large brass key into the lock and turned it.

The door opened out onto a pleasant little room, though dark. Holmes strode across and opened the curtains allowing light to flood into the room. The furniture was old, but well kept. A small bookcase laden with books sat against one wall, with an overstuffed armchair seated beneath the window to take advantage of good light for reading. The book case contained mainly books upon the subject of law, along with Henry Mayhew's "London Labour and the London Poor" and several works by Charles Dickens. Peter Harrington had clearly been a man with a social conscience.

To the left of the armchair sat a small writing desk and chair.

A door to the right of the entrance led into a small, but seemingly comfortable, bedroom. A large iron bedstead dominated the room. Warm woolen rugs dotted the floor. An oaken blanket box sat at the end of the bed. Situated in front of a small window was a table with a plain porcelain ewer and basin for washing, resting on top of it. A small polished wooden box, no doubt containing shaving implements, also sat on the table next to a small mirror.

A quick look around the bedroom, and in the blanket box, soon convinced Holmes that there was little of interest to be found, and he turned his attention to the sitting room and to the desk, seating himself before it. He attempted to open it, only to find it was locked. "Hmmm. Harrington kept his desk locked."

"Unusual, don't you think, Mr. Holmes?" said Crawford, inspecting the keys he held, obviously looking for the key to the desk.

"I would not make too much out it, inspector. A prudent man locks his desk. Maids are notoriously curious," Holmes replied.

Crawford selected a small key and held it out to Holmes, who took it and inserted it into the lock. There was a small click and Holmes opened the desk, handing the key back to Crawford as he did so.

"A prudent man, and a methodical one," Holmes commented as he took in the neatly arrayed contents of the desk.

I contented myself with gazing around the room, attempting to get a feel for its former occupant whilst Holmes perused the contents of the desk. I was most definitely not as good at it as Holmes, as all I could see was that Harrington had been a young man with a social conscience, and an orderly mind as evinced by the neatness of his desk, but nothing else caught my attention. The room was tidy and clean, but that was most likely due to the maid, not Harrington. No photographs or works of art adorned the walls. I would have expected to see a photograph of Miss Leadbetter at the very least.

"Hmmm. Well, now, this is interesting." Holmes' voice drew me from my thoughts.

I turned to look at Holmes' discovery. He held what appeared to be a note written on extremely good quality writing paper. Gazing over his shoulder I read: "Come to the Prince's Barrow at 2 o'clock tomorrow." The note was unsigned and also undated.

Crawford read the note over Holmes' other shoulder. "Prince's Barrow is where Harrington was found," he commented. "It is called that because it is quite a small barrow and the locals believe it was the burial chamber of a minor Anglo-Saxon prince. It is much older than that, however, according to Sir Denby at least. And it is on Sir Denby Hardcastle's estate."

"But who did the note come from?" I asked.

"That is something for us to discover, my dear Watson," Holmes replied, carefully folding the note and tucking it into his coat pocket. "It is written in what is clearly a feminine hand. I do find it curious, however, that the note is unsigned."

"An illicit meeting?" Crawford asked.

"Not necessarily," Holmes replied. "It could simply be that Harrington was so familiar with the handwriting that the writer did not need to sign it."

"From someone like Verity Leadbetter?" I asked.

"It is certainly a possibility, Watson. No doubt we shall find out in due course."

"A tryst with a lady, perhaps?" suggested Inspector Crawford.

"Again, it is a possibility. Until I have more facts, however, I refuse to theorize. When one does that, inevitably one begins to twist the facts to suit the theory."

I could see Inspector Crawford absorbing that thought, head tilted slightly to one side. He nodded acceptance of Holmes' dictum, then looked around the room. "I cannot see that there are any more facts to find here."

Holmes cast his sharp gaze once more around the room. "I agree, inspector, apart from the note, I think that this particular well is dry."

We took our leave from the household. The maid, Harriet, seemed pleased to see us go. We walked back to the offices of Somerville and Cannon to return the keys. Holmes showed Mr. Somerville the note.

The gentleman scrutinized the paper for a moment, then shook his head and handed it back to my friend. "I am sorry, gentlemen, but the writing is unfamiliar to me."

Holmes tucked the note back into his pocket. "I was almost certain that it would be, but it would have been remiss of me not to enquire."

We all shook hands with Mr. Somerville and left the premises. As we stood beside the trap, Inspector Crawford asked "Where to now, Mr. Holmes?"

"Back to Barrow-upon-Kennet, I think. I do not believe we can accomplish anything further here in Marlborough," Holmes replied. "At least, not today. I may need to return at a later date. The scene of the death is near the village, and that, I am sure, is where our killer, if indeed there is one, is to be found."

We climbed into the trap, the driver clucked the reigns, and the pony began his wearisome work of returning us to Barrow-upon-Kennet.

Holmes sat in silence for a while, whilst I once again drank in the bucolic charms of Wiltshire. After about fifteen minutes. Holmes turned to Inspector Crawford. "You said you were born in Barrow-upon-Kennet?"

"Yes, Mr. Holmes. My father was Sir Matthew Hardcastle's coachman. My eldest brother now holds that position with Sir Matthew's son, Sir Denby Hardcastle."

"Excellent. No doubt you can tell us about the inhabitants of Barrow Hill Manor."

"Of course. What would you like to know?"

"Whatever you can tell me about those who live there and their frequent visitors," Holmes replied.

"Everyone? Including the servants?" Inspector Crawford's eyebrows arched in amusement.

Holmes gave a wry smile. "That would be a formidable task, would it not? Start with the family and their friends. We can expand to the servants if it becomes necessary. Which it may very well do."

"Very well, Mr. Holmes." Inspector Crawford paused to gather his thoughts. "Sir Denby Hardcastle is Sir Matthew's second son and a bit of an odd bird."

"Second son?" I asked, turning my attention to the conversation.

"Yes. Sir Denby was much overlooked as a child. Left very much to his own devices, quiet and bookish, indeed his father took little notice of him. There was talk, my father said, of sending him to Cambridge or Oxford and then steering him into the church. That plan fell apart when his older brother, Montgomery, fell off his horse into the duck pond whilst drunk and drowned."

Holmes raised his eyebrows. "An accident?"

"I believe so. It was certainly never treated as if it could possibly be anything else," the inspector replied.

Holmes hummed to himself and waved to Crawford to continue.

"Sir Denby is married to Lady Augusta."

"We have been told that the lady is an American," I said.

"That is so, Doctor Watson." Inspector Crawford's face took on a slightly sour expression. "The lady is not well-regarded in these parts."

"Why ever not?" I asked.

"Lady Augusta is brash and outspoken, with little feel for the conventions of village life," Crawford replied. "The lady has alienated almost everyone in Barrow-upon-Kennet. I think the only people who still talk to her, beyond the necessities of politeness, are Reverend Browning, his wife, and his daughter. Their daughter, Hyacinth Browning is a regular visitor to the manor."

Holmes raised his eyebrows. "It is a little unusual to find a vicar's daughter socializing with the gentry," he commented.

Inspector Crawford sighed. "Hyacinth Browning is a strange girl. The worst sort of romantic with her head filled with fluff and dreams. John Wright describes her as having 'a head full of dandelion fluff', and he isn't wrong. The girl seems to be a little simple. A nice enough lass, but doesn't seem capable of following a simple thought from beginning to end, let alone a complex one. That is why when Lady Augusta started her society, if seemed odd that Miss Browning was the first to join."

"Society?" I asked.

"The Society of Ancient Virtues," Crawford replied with a grimace.

"What are the aims of this society? Surely it would not have many members?"

"You would be surprised, doctor, what people will do to avoid boredom," said Crawford.

I refrained from looking at Holmes. "I am well acquainted with how some people handle ennui."

"If you are not a person into riding to hounds, or painting watercolours, or any other rural pursuit, there isn't a great deal to do around here," Crawford continued. "After the birth of her children, Lady Augusta was looking around for a pastime. She found nothing that suited her, so she created her own."

"She created her own society?" Holmes' tone expressed his surprise at the audacity of this action.

"Yes. Lady Augusta is very taken with the ancient Romans and the virtues they were so proud of."

"Gravitas, dignitas, and the like?" I asked, dragging my memory for my minimal Latin, which was mostly comprised of medical terms.

"Yes, doctor. The members of the society meet several times a month at Barrow Hill Manor. Though several of the members are living in the manor almost permanently. What the society actually does is a matter of conjecture."

"These members being the friends you will tell us about?"

"Yes, Mr. Holmes."

"Pray continue."

"I have mentioned Hyacinth Browning. Peter Harrington was a member, as is Verity Leadbetter, whom you have met."

"Is Algernon Leadbetter a member?" I asked.

"No, doctor. I don't believe our esteemed Member of Parliament cares much for Sir Denby and Lady Augusta. He only socializes with them when he absolutely has to. Though it may very well be Sir Francis Cigne that he does not like. I will get to Sir Francis shortly."

I nodded.

"Another member is Mrs. Celeste Feuer. She is a youngish widow. Also American. The lady is a long-time friend of Lady Augusta's. Mrs. Feuer came to Barrow Hill Manor after the death of her husband, a German industrialist, three years ago, and never left. According to my brother the staff do not know how to treat the lady. She is neither really family nor yet staff. She fills the role of companion to Lady Augusta, but is definitely not paid to be such." Inspector Crawford paused for breath. "Then there is Mr. Tobermoray Flyte. He is a retired banker. Somewhat portly and rather hearty in his opinions. No-one seems to know what his connection to the manor is. He arrived to stay at the invitation of Sir Matthew and has never left."

Inspector Crawford was silent for a moment. "The final member is Sir Francis Cigne. He is a rather dissolute young man. There was some scandal in London and his family rusticated him. He refused to return to his family home in Melksham, and came here instead. At Lady Augusta's invitation, so gossip has it."

"Scandal?" Holmes looked at Crawford.

"Yes, Mr. Holmes. I do not know the details."

Holmes waved a hand. "No matter. I am sure my brother will be able to obtain the details."

"Is it really pertinent, Holmes?" I asked. I found the idea of gossip distasteful.

"At this point, my dear doctor, I have no idea what information will prove pertinent to the case." Holmes looked at Crawford. "Pray continue."

"That is really all there is, Mr. Holmes. Without the servants, of course."

"Children?" Holmes asked.

"Ah, yes. Sir Denby and Lady Augusta have three children. The heir, Henry is twelve. Augustus is ten, and Elspeth is eight. Henry has gone away to school. Rugby, I think. The two youngest are in the care of a nanny, a frightfully formidable Scots woman. I cannot see how the children could possibly pertain to Harrington's death, Mr. Holmes."

"They most likely do not, inspector. What they are, however, is background detail. You never know when such details will prove to be of use."

Inspector Crawford chuckled drily. "Well, I give you fair warning, Mr. Holmes, don't try and use the children. The nanny will eat you for breakfast. She is fiercely protective of her charges, so my brother says."

"Duly noted," Holmes replied with equal dryness.

We lapsed into silence for a while. The village was coming into sight when Inspector Crawford asked "When do you want to visit the manor, Mr. Holmes?"

Holmes shrugged lightly. "Now is as good a time as any."

Crawford leaned forward and tapped the driver on the shoulder. "Make for Barrow Hill Manor, Fred."

The driver nodded tersely, guiding the pony around the village green and onto the road leading out of the village and up the hill, towards the manor house I had glimpsed upon our arrival in Barrow-upon-Kennet the previous day.

Chapter Five

Barrow Hill Manor was a fine house built in the Jacobean style of local stone and flint. It looked both sombre and imposing. The front was gabled as were the two wings abutting it. Huge casement windows gave views sweeping down towards the village. This was a house with a sense of history. One felt that it had sat there for centuries, watching silently over the village below with benign dignity.

A smartly dressed butler came out onto the front steps as the trap drew to a stop. He was tall and saturnine, with dark hair that was touched with silver, and with a long nose that he looked down towards us. When he spoke his voice was cold and just this side of polite. "What do you do here, Jimmy?"

Irritation crossed Crawford's face. His tone matched the butler's exactly. "I am here to see Sir Denby and Lady Augusta in my official capacity as an Inspector of the Wiltshire Constabulary. We are investigating the death of Peter Harrington."

"That death had nothing to do with my master and his lady." The butler's tone got even colder.

"It occurred on their land, Featherstone, and that alone is reason enough for my presence."

Featherstone sniffed. "And these gentlemen?"

"Mr. Sherlock Holmes and Doctor John Watson, from London."

Featherstone's eyes widened slightly at the mention of my friend's name, and he turned a little grey. "You had best come in, then. I shall inform Sir Denby of your arrival."

We followed the butler through the imposing front entrance into the coolness of the atrium. He left as there and disappeared into the bowels of the house.

"That was interesting, was it not, Watson?" Holmes murmured in my ear. "Featherstone seems to be the very epitome of butlerdom. I do wonder what little secrets that charming fellow does not wish revealed. He was certainly more nervous than he had wont to be." Holmes raised his voice then. "Mr. Featherstone seems not to care for you, Inspector," he observed.

Inspector Crawford pursed his lips. When he spoke, his tone was gruff. "The staff, the senior staff at least, remember me as one of the coachman's brats. I am sure Featherstone thinks I should use the tradesmen's entrance, but I am damned if I am going to be bullied by him. There is the dignity of the Wiltshire Constabulary to consider after all."

"Indeed," Holmes muttered in response.

Featherstone reappeared. "Sir Denby will see you now."

We were conducted through labyrinthine hallways to a study at the rear of the manor. One wall contained large windows that looked out towards a vista of groves of trees, a large duck pond, on which I noted that there were several swans paddling serenely, along with a number of somewhat noisy ducks, and, in the near distance, a barrow. I wondered if this were the barrow that had been mentioned in the note that Holmes had found.

A large mahogany desk was situated to take advantage of the light from the windows, and to have a line of sight to the door. The surrounding walls where lined with bookshelves and display cases. I noticed what appeared to be tear drop-shaped lumps of stone in the nearest case. Several comfortable looking chairs dotted the room, and a small sideboard stood in a corner behind the desk. Also standing behind the desk was a genial looking man in his mid-forties.

The man's hair was dark blonde and receding slightly at the temples. Cool blue eyes gazed at us curiously, though somewhat dispassionately. He came around the desk and held out his hand. "Gentlemen, welcome to Barrow Hill Manor, I am Sir Denby Hardcastle. It is a great pleasure to meet the famous Mr. Sherlock Holmes and Doctor John Watson."

Sir Denby flicked a glance at Featherstone. "Thank you, Featherstone. That will be all." The butler bowed slightly and left the room.

Sir Denby shook first Holmes' hand and then mine, before clasping Inspector Crawford on the shoulder. "A pleasure to see you again, Jimmy. I was only asking your brother about you last week. He said you were living in Devizes." Sir Denby crossed to the small sideboard behind the desk and extracted a decanter and four glasses.

"I am, Sir Denby," Crawford replied, "but seeing as I know the area, the Commissioner felt I was the best person to handle the investigation into Mr. Harrington's untimely death."

Sir Denby paused in the midst of pouring drinks. He glanced over his shoulder at Crawford, eyebrows raised slightly. "I thought that Peter's death was declared to be an accident?"

"Mr. Leadbetter believes otherwise," the inspector said.

"Hence the involvement of these august gentlemen." Sir Denby nodded his understanding of the situation. "Well, I cannot say I blame Algernon for being concerned. Peter was to marry little Verity, after all."

Sir Denby handed us all glasses of what, after a discreet sniff, I realized was a very decent whisky. I took a tentative sip. It was a little early in the day for spirits, but one must be polite, after all.

Holmes sipped his whisky for a moment, then set the glass upon the desk. "There are one or two points about Mr. Harrington's death that are of interest. I was only too happy, therefore, to accede to Mr. Leadbetter's request for Mr. Harrington's death to be properly investigated."

Inspector Crawford winced at Holmes' last words, and I could not, in all honesty, blame him. I turned my attention back to the glass cases filled with lumps of rock, to avoid watching Crawford's embarrassment.

Sir Denby swirled his drink around. "I see," he said thoughtfully. "Naturally, you want my assistance."

"Of course, Mr. Harrington's body was found on your land, after all."

"Yes," Sir Denby sighed, "...it was. Of course I will assist in any manner that I can. You may go where you will in the manor." His tone changed. "You are admiring my collection, Doctor Watson?"

"Indeed, Sir Denby. It is a most interesting display." I had no idea what I was looking at.

"The tools of our prehistoric ancestors." He came to stand beside me. Taking a ring of keys from his pocket, he opened the nearest case and extracted one of the vaguely triangular stones and placed it reverently in my hand.

Involuntarily, my hand clenched around it. It was, I could now see, a piece of flint, carefully worked to have a sharp edge, and to fit snuggly into the palm of one's hand.

"That tool, doctor, was created around 12,000 years ago. A man like you, or I, used this to cut up his captured prey. To skin it. To joint it for cooking. Is it not an amazing thought?"

I turned the rock over in my hand, barely listening to Sir Denby enthusing in my ear. I was wondering at the work that had gone in to this primitive but effective tool. Holmes stepped up to join us. He had been examining Sir Denby's bookshelves. I handed the object to him. He examined it closely.

"A marvellous thing indeed, Sir Denby," Holmes said. "This comes from around here?"

"Oh yes, Mr. Holmes. My entire collection of hand axes, spear heads, and blades comes from this estate and its environs. I started collecting them when I was a boy. The one that you hold was found in the Prince's Barrow, as the locals call it. It is most certainly not an Anglo-Saxon burial cairn, but from a much earlier period. Probably around 9,000 to 3,500 B.C. The era termed 'Neolithic' by John Lubbock." Sir Denby paused for breath. "We owe much to that gentleman," he continued. "John Lubbock purchased the Avebury circle to stop that glorious religious site of our ancestors being torn down for mere building material."

Sir Denby looked out of the window at the barrow. "Are you gentlemen familiar with West Kennet Long Barrow?" he asked, not waiting for a response. "The Prince's Barrow is much like West Kennet Long Barrow but on a decidedly smaller scale. John Thurnham's excavation of the West Kennet site in 1859 showed it to be Neolithic. Thurnham was medical superintendent at the county asylum. He used patients from the asylum as workers on the site. Said it was excellent occupational therapy. Remarkable man. I made similar finds to his in our barrow. Not as many, of course. But there is no doubt in my mind that both barrows were built by the same people for much the same reasons."

I perceived that Sir Denby was more than a little enthusiastic about his chosen subject. Not unlike Holmes in that respect. I smiled to myself.

"A very fine thing to do," said Holmes. "We can learn much from the past."

Sir Denby smiled delightedly at my friend's comment.

"Indeed we can, sir," said a female voice from the doorway, "...but the brutish prehistoric past cannot teach us as much as classical antiquity can."

Sir Denby took the hand axe from Holmes and turned back towards the case it belonged in. I thought his shoulders slumped slightly.

Holmes and I turned towards the entrance.

A woman stood in the doorway looking at us. She was quite tall. Being almost my own height. The lady had a heart-shaped face, aquiline nose, pale-blue eyes that looked at Sir Denby with an expression of mild contempt, and abundant blonde hair piled in an elaborate chignon. She was dressed fairly expensively, though her clothes were a trifle outdated in style, as if the lady did not much mix with society. This was a woman whom one would describe as handsome, rather than beautiful.

She stepped into the room, and addressed Sir Denby. "Featherstone said we had visitors. You were going to bring them to meet me, were you not?"

The lady's voice held both mild reproach and the hint of an American accent. I realized that this must be Lady Augusta.

"The gentlemen are here on business, Augusta."

"Business?"

"They are investigating Peter's death."

Lady Augusta looked at us, then smiled. "James. I did not see you there. You are investigating poor Peter's death?"

Inspector Crawford, I noticed, had attempted to conceal himself in a corner. He looked wary. He shook his head slightly. "No, Lady Augusta, I am here to provide official assistance to these gentlemen." Crawford gestured to us. "Lady Augusta, may I present Mr. Sherlock Holmes and Doctor John Watson, from London."

Lady Augusta extended a hand graciously. "It is an honour to meet you gentlemen. I have heard of you both. Word of your marvellous abilities has reached here, Mr. Holmes. Sir Francis has told me about the events at Lord Robert St. Simon's wedding last year."

"Sir Francis is a friend of Lord Robert?" I asked. I was surprised, for the little I had heard of Sir Francis Cigne did not lend me to imagine him as friends with the somewhat stand-offish, stick-in-the-mud that was Lord Robert St. Simon.

"Sir Francis is acquainted with a lady named Flora Millar, who I believe is a friend of Lord Robert's."

Miss Flora Millar was many things, but by no stretch of the imagination could that feisty young woman be considered a lady. I pondered a suitable response.

Lady Augusta then stepped between Holmes and I, hooking her arms through ours, in a gesture of familiarity that, I freely admit, somewhat shocked me.

"You really must come and meet the others," she said. "I am holding a meeting of the Society of Ancient Virtues and most of the other members are staying here. Though dear Verity is unable to attend, being in mourning for poor Peter, of course. And Hyacinth was needed at home today. But I am sure the others will be thrilled to meet you. And I am equally sure that the grandeur and accomplishments of the Roman Empire are of far more interest to such sophisticated gentlemen as yourselves, than my husband's mouldering primitives and their pathetic rocks."

I cast a quizzical glance at Holmes above Lady Augusta's head. Holmes dropped one eyelid in a quick wink, asking me, without words, to play along.

He turned his attention to Lady Augusta. "And I am sure Watson and myself will be equally thrilled to make their acquaintance. Just as we have been to make yours, dear lady." His tone held just enough admiration and an air of gallantry to be convincing without being overly effusive. I was reminded once again that the stage had lost a talented actor when Holmes decided to become the world's only consulting detective.

Lady Augusta laughed delightedly and swept us out of the room, and into the hallway, then up a sweeping and elegant flight of stairs to a wide mezzanine that was flanked with rows of suits of armour. Inspector Crawford followed behind us, somewhat reluctantly, I felt. We went past the suits of armour, and around to the right of the mezzanine, to where a door opened into what was obviously a large drawing room. The paintings on the walls – still lifes of flowers fruit and such objects, the light fabric of the drapes, and the vases full of summer flowers, gave the impression that this was an exclusively feminine domain.

Two men and another woman were seated in chairs near a large window. I could see the Prince's Barrow through the window and realized that this room must be directly above Sir Denby's study.

The woman was around Lady Augusta's age. She was dressed in a less opulent manner than Lady Augusta, in a more restrained style that was similar to that I had seen on German women visiting London. Her dress was a dove-grey colour that made her look pale and washed out. The lady had soft brown hair drawn back into a tight bun. She also had soft doe-like brown eyes that held a depth of sadness. I realized that this must be the friend and unofficial companion of whom Inspector Crawford had spoken.

"Mr. Sherlock Holmes, Doctor John Watson, may I present to you my dear friend, Mrs. Celeste Feuer?" The sad lady rose from her seat and gave us the briefest of smiles, and dipped a small curtsey. We both smiled politely at her, nodding a greeting.

"This is Mr. Tobermoray Flyte.," continued Lady Augusta.

A somewhat rotund older man, with greying hair and the ruddy complexion of a man who enjoys the finer things of life, and is possibly paying for that enjoyment with heart troubles and gout, rose to his feet and shook our hands. "A pleasure to meet you, gentlemen." His voice was as hearty as his complexion and his handshake firm.

"Likewise," I murmured. Holmes nodded his agreement.

"And finally, this is Sir Francis Cigne." Our hostess's voice dropped into what could almost be described as a coo.

We turned our attention to the last of the trio. He was a tall young man, with dark eyes, ebony curls, and an air of complete dissipation, who rose languidly to his feet and waved a hand in our direction. "Charmed, I am sure. I have heard of you, Mr. Holmes. What brings a man of your undoubted intellect to this benighted hole?"

I could not forebear raising my eyebrows at the insult to his host's home.

"Death, Sir Francis," my friend replied, ignoring the young man's insolence.

"You don't mean Harrington's death, surely?" Sir Francis exclaimed. "That was an accident."

"Was it?"

"Of course, it was. What else could it have been?"

"That is what we are here to find out," Holmes replied.

"Nonsense!" snorted Sir Francis.

"It was a damned odd death, is what it was," Tobermoray Flyte interjected. "Police were damned useless. Police are always damned useless. Impertinent as well."

Out of the corner of my eye, I saw Inspector Crawford cringe, and Holmes make a note of Flyte's odd comment.

My friend turned his attention back to Lady Augusta. "You will forgive us, I trust, if we do not stay. We have much to do."

"Of course, Mr. Holmes. You and Doctor Watson are welcome here at any time. In fact, you must come and dine with us."

I noted that James Crawford was not included in the invitation. I looked to where he was standing in the doorway. The inspector gave me a wry smile, obviously following my line of thought.

We took our leave and joined Crawford in the corridor. Featherstone loomed out of nowhere to conduct us to the front door, obviously not trusting us to find our own way out.

As we headed back towards the main entrance, Holmes paused beside one of the suits of armour. I noted he was carefully inspecting one of the gauntlets. "A fine suit of armour," he commented. "A family heirloom, no doubt?"

"Alas no, sir," replied Featherstone. "The Hardcastle family is not of sufficient venerability to have owned such things. The suits of armour were purchased by Sir Denby's grandfather, Sir Montgomery. That gentleman was of the opinion that there was no finer item of decoration than arms and armour. If you have an interest in such things, perhaps you would care to ask Sir Denby to show you the collection of pikes and swords that are housed in the library and billiard room." The butler paused. "If it is the medieval period itself that interests you, there is also a selection of works on heraldry and medieval symbolism in the library collection. They also belonged to Sir Montgomery. He was very interested in that period of history."

"Thank you, my good fellow, I shall do exactly that," Holmes replied jovially.

I wondered what Holmes was up to, having never seen him exhibit the slightest interest in the history of anything apart from sensational crime.

Chapter Six

We were silent during the short trip back to the village. Holmes' faux jocularity had given way to his more normal introspection. I drank in the surrounding beauty, and Inspector Crawford stared somewhat morosely at the floor of the trap.

Arriving at the Wight and Barrel, we paused briefly to inquire about the possibility of a late lunch, which Mr. Wright assured us was perfectly possible, and then the three of us retired to Holmes and my rooms to await our repast.

Mrs. Wright delivered a tray of sandwiches, cold hard-boiled eggs, salad, and a pot of good, strong tea. Nothing of substance was said until after we had eaten our fill.

At last, Inspector Crawford set his cup and saucer down upon the table and said, "Well, gentlemen, what do we do now?"

Holmes frowned slightly, taking a sip of his tea. "Are you able to obtain for me copies of both the police report and the post-mortem report on Peter Harrington?"

Inspector Crawford shrugged his shoulders. "I don't see why not. I was instructed to give you all the assistance that you required."

"Excellent. I should like to acquaint myself with exactly what has been established, or, at the very least, surmised, until now."

"I should quite like to read the post-mortem report as well," I said.

Holmes nodded. "Your professional opinion, my dear Watson, would be greatly appreciated."

Crawford got to his feet. "I shall head back to Devizes, then. It may take me a day or two to lay my hands on the reports."

"We shall confine ourselves the village and its surroundings, and await your return. I should like to take a close look at this Prince's Barrow."

Crawford nodded. "I shall leave you gentlemen to it, then."

"One moment, Inspector, if you please," Holmes said. "I shall give you the address of my brother in London. If you could telegraph him to obtain the details of the Sir Francis Cigne scandal, I would be grateful. This village is too small to have a telegraph office."

"Even if it did have an office," I observed, "given the nature of villages would you want our business to be the subject of local gossip?"

"Indeed. If you wish to know what is going on in any community you have only to inquire of the publican, the post master, and the telegraph office," replied Holmes.

Crawford nodded his agreement and wrote Mycroft's name and the address of the Diogenes Club into his notebook as Holmes dictated them to him. He then picked up the lunch tray and disappeared down the stairs.

I wandered to the window and watched as the inspector exited the building, climbed into the waiting trap, and was driven away. I turned back into the room. Holmes had withdrawn the note he had found in Harrington's rooms from his pocket and was studying it intently.

"Well, Holmes?" I asked.

"It is clearly the handwriting of a woman," Holmes replied. "You see the swirls and flourishes on the capital letters?"

I peered over his shoulder and hummed somewhat noncommittedly.

"This note, my dear Watson, was written by a woman of strong character and determination. She knows what she wants. There is no hesitancy at all in the writing. No small blots or droplets to mark where the pen has left the page mid word. Which also denotes a good quality pen. Many of the cheaper ones do tend to splutter and make a mess of the paper."

Holmes turned the paper towards the light from the window. "The paper is of very good quality as well. Reminiscent of the quality papers turned out by Dobbs Kidd and Company. No watermark, however. But that could have been cut off. You see that the bottom of the paper is uneven? It has been cut with scissors; ones with small blades, quite possibly embroidery scissors."

"But who is the note from, Holmes?"

"A good question, Watson. And one that I do not as yet have an answer for."

"Could it be from a client?" I asked.

"I find that suggestion extremely unlikely. It would be a strange client indeed that sent an anonymous note asking to meet in such an odd place. With one of my clients that may, perhaps, be a possibility, but highly unlikely for the client of a junior lawyer. No, Watson, I suspect this is a billet-doux."

"A love letter?" I was startled. "A strange place for an assignation," I observed. "You can see the barrow quite clearly from the manor." I thought for a moment. "So Inspector Crawford was right, it was an illicit meeting."

Holmes shook his head. "Not necessarily, Watson. This note may have been written by Miss Leadbetter."

"You will ask her?"

"In time, my friend, and maybe not directly. If it was an illicit meeting, as you put it, there is no purpose to be served by distressing the lady further."

Holmes carefully folded the note and tucked it away in his travelling case. I sat in a chair near the window for a while thinking over the visit to Barrow Hill Manor. A thought struck me. "Holmes?"

"Hmmm?" came the distracted reply.

"Since when have you been interested in arms and armour?"

"Only since I noted the scratches on the gauntlet of that suit of armour at the manor today," Holmes replied drily.

"Scratches?"

"Yes, Watson. The palm and fingers of the right hand gauntlet of that particular suit of armour had quite deep horizontal scratches."

"How on earth did you notice them?"

"That gauntlet was cleaner than its left hand counterpart. The juxtaposition of it caught my eye."

"Is it related to the case?"

Holmes shrugged. "It may be nothing more than an unusually incompetent housemaid. At this point, however, any oddity, no matter how small, may prove to be of interest."

He crossed the room and took the seat opposite me. "Well, my friend, what did you make of the people we met today? A motley collection of individuals, do not you think?"

I laughed. "Motley indeed."

"What did you make of Sir Denby?"

"He appeared to be an honest man. A trifle eccentric with his love of all things prehistoric."

"He is something of a scholar on the subject," Holmes commented. "I noted all nine volumes of 'The Itinerary of John Leland, The Antiquary' edited by Thomas Hearne and published last century, as well as the more modern works of John Lubbock: 'Prehistoric Times as Illustrated by Ancient Remains' and 'Antiquity of Man.'"

"A scholar indeed," I agreed. "But there seems to be no harm in him. He was certainly agreeable to our presence."

"And his charming wife?"

"I understand now what your brother meant about the lady."

"Yes, she is certainly a force of nature, is she not?"

"Maybe too much of one for a truly happy marriage," I said.

"You mean the way Sir Denby visibly deflated when his wife entered the room?" Holmes shrugged. "It is not uncommon, my friend. Marriages amongst the gentry and the nobility are rarely love matches. The most that can be hoped for is friendship."

"I do not think that marriage has even that."

"We saw them together for only a few minutes, Watson," Holmes reminded me. "Not long enough to judge the true state of affairs."

"True," I sighed.

"And what of the other lady we met?"

"Mrs. Celeste Feuer? She seemed to be a rather sad, somewhat pathetic figure."

Holmes nodded. "The lady has gone from being the wife of an industrialist to what appears to be unpaid companion to Lady Augusta. There is a story there, and a somewhat sad one, I think."

I nodded my agreement with my friend's assessment. "The two men are very different, are they not?"

"They are indeed. Tobermoray Flyte is every inch the retired city gent." Holmes frowned. "His little rant about the police was decidedly odd."

"Could he be the killer?"

"Far too early to tell, Watson." Holmes' tone held a note of mild reproof. "He may simply have had an unhappy experience with them that has left him jaded. Many people do."

I nodded my agreement.

"Sir Francis Cigne, on the other hand," continued Holmes, "strikes me as the worst sort of bounder. There is something deeply unpleasant about that young man, Watson."

I thought about it for a moment. "You are correct, Holmes. I think he is what our grandparents would have termed a rake."

"You may very well be right," Holmes agreed. "It takes a great deal in the way of scandal to get a young man rusticated from society, especially London society. They have vastly different standards in the counties. Usually much higher ones." Holmes frowned. "It has been my experience that that level of scandal usually takes the form of the wrong sort of woman."

"Consorting with prostitutes?"

Holmes shook his head. "No. That is almost expected of a dashing young man about town. The sort of scandal that sees young men ejected from polite society usually involves the wives or daughters of their hosts."

"Do you think Mycroft will know?"

"If he does not, then he will know where to obtain the information," Holmes replied.

"What of Featherstone?" I asked.

"The erstwhile butler. A bit of a snob, but that is not uncommon amongst upper house servants. He seemed more than a little put out to see us. I would even go so far as to say that he was fearful."

"Could that fear be tied into Harrington's death?"

Holmes waggled his hand from side to side, indicating maybe yes, maybe no. "It could be nothing more than a guilty conscience rising from skimming the household accounts, or chasing the maid servants."

I smiled slightly at the image of the terribly correct Featherstone chasing a maid around the parlour.

Holmes continued, "But, again, it is something to take note of. Tell me, Watson, what did you make of Inspector Crawford?"

"He seems a pleasant enough chap." I thought back to Lady Augusta's appearance in her husband's study. "Though I thought he seemed a little afraid of Lady Augusta."

"The way he shrank back into the corner?" Holmes gave a dry little chuckle. "Not really surprising, my friend. I am sure that good lady has frightened more men than the inspector has." He frowned again. "I am intrigued by this Society of Ancient Virtues that Crawford said existed."

"Sir Francis Cigne does not strike me as the type to be interested in any virtues, ancient or otherwise," I commented.

"A good point. We also need to meet the last member of the society."

"Last member?"

"Come Watson, surely you have not forgotten that Crawford told us that the vicar's daughter was involved."

"Oh. Yes. It did seem odd, when he mentioned it."

"I think it is time for another walk around the village." He rose to his feet and glanced at his fob watch. "Not too early to call in upon the vicar and introduce ourselves. Shall we?" Holmes gestured towards the door. Nodding my acquiescence, I rose to my feet, gathered my coat, and followed Holmes from the room.

Chapter Seven

Outside, I was struck again by the simple beauty of the village. It seemed a gentle, calm place where the cares of the world could simply slip away. Holmes and I walked around the green towards the church. As we approached, a tall middle-aged man in a cassock emerged from the church, locked the door behind him, and came down the steps. When he saw us, he stopped and waited for us to approach.

"Good afternoon," said Holmes. "You must be the vicar of this fair parish."

"Good afternoon to you, Mr. Holmes, Doctor Watson," the gentleman replied.

At my look of surprise, the reverend gentleman chuckled softly. "Barrow-upon-Kennet is a small village, doctor. Any visitors tend to stand out. And when the visitors are as well-known as the eminent detective Mr. Sherlock Holmes and his erstwhile companion, Doctor John Watson, well, I doubt the village will stop talking about your visit for years."

"You know, of course, why we are here?" Holmes asked softly.

The vicar nodded sadly. "The death of poor Peter Harrington." He shook himself. "I am both rude and remiss. I have not introduced myself. Simon Browning, vicar of this parish, at your service. Come inside and meet my family. I am sure that you were coming to talk to me, so we may as well do this in comfort."

Reverend Browning led the way into the manse. A maid was sent scurrying for her mistress and to arrange tea. The vicar led us into a cosy parlour, with a view that looked out into a small garden. We sat in comfortable, but faded armchairs.

The small cat we had seen the previous day sauntered in, inspected us both closely, and then went to the vicar for a chin scratch, which he duly supplied. The vicar looked up at us with a small smile from where he was bent over the cat. "This is Belle. My daughter obtained her from the manor. She was the runt of the litter and the stable man was going to drown her. We had tears and tantrums before my wife agreed to take the cat. My daughter is very soft-hearted." Belle shrugged herself free of the vicar's hand and leaped up upon the window ledge to lay in the sun.

"You have a fine church," Holmes observed. "Fourteenth century?"

"Yes. Though there has been a church here since Saxon times. You are a student of church architecture, Mr. Holmes?"

"One picks up all sorts of knowledge in the course of one's business. I once had a case that hinged on the age of the narthex of a small church." Holmes glanced at me. "This was before your time, Watson."

"You must tell me about it sometime, Holmes. It sounds like a fascinating case," I replied.

The squeak of a tea trolley heralded the arrival of the maid, accompanied by a lady of similar age to the vicar. She was short, slender, and perhaps best described as mousy. Her countenance was anxious; her eyes darting looks at us, as if she were prepared to run if we made too quick a move.

We rose politely to our feet. Reverend Browning took her hand. "Cynthia, my dear, I would like to introduce to you Mr. Sherlock Holmes and Doctor John Watson." He turned to us. "Gentlemen, this is my wife, Mrs. Cynthia Browning." He looked over his wife's shoulder, towards the door, eyebrows raised, "And where is Hyacinth?"

Mrs. Browning sighed. "Up at the manor. Again."

Reverend Browning's lips pulled into a thin, tight line. "That girl spends far too much time up there."

"Lady Augusta encourages her. She told me how delightful it was to find a young girl so interested in the glories of Rome rather than chasing young men."

The reverend's lips tightened further. I exchanged a quick glance with Holmes. Obviously something was not right here.

Reverend Browning sighed and changed the subject. "Will you take tea with us, my dear?"

His wife patted his shoulder. "No. I shall pour for you and then leave you gentlemen to your discussion. I am sure it has to do with poor Peter Harrington's death, and that is not something I feel I can contribute to."

"Did you know Mr. Harrington, ma'am?" asked Holmes.

"I had met him. He, like our Hyacinth, was a member of the Society of Ancient Virtues," Mrs. Browning replied. "I formed the impression that he was more a member for Miss Leadbetter's sake, than due to any true interest of his own in the subject. Though I am sure it did him no harm in his career to associate with the gentry." The lady poured the tea for us, then took her leave.

We settled back in our chairs. The good reverend's face was somewhat shuttered. He sighed again. "Forgive me my bad temper, gentlemen, there is something about that society of Lady Augusta's that does not sit well with me."

Holmes leaned forward. "And what would that be?"

Reverend Browning shook his head. "I cannot put it into words, for I have not been able to put my finger on exactly what is wrong. The members mostly strike a wrong note with me. You know how it is."

"Dissembling can take many forms," Holmes agreed blandly. "We have heard a little of this society from Inspector Crawford."

"There isn't much to tell, Mr. Holmes. According to my daughter, they meet, have tea, and discuss the glories of Rome, with the accent upon the virtues."

"How long has this society being going?" I asked.

"About seven months."

Holmes raised his eyebrows. "I would not have thought that antique virtues could generate an entire seven months' worth of conversation."

Reverend Browning smiled wanly. "I believe they also discuss Roman literature and architecture."

"That is a discussion that could last a good while," Holmes agreed. "How long has your daughter been a member?"

"Hyacinth has been going up to the manor for several years. My daughter was a very pretty child and Lady Augusta was very taken with her when she first arrived. Made something of a pet of her. As Hyacinth approached womanhood, Lady Augusta took her under her wing. There really isn't much chance of Hyacinth making a suitable marriage here, and Lady Augusta offered to groom her and find her a suitable husband. I believe the lady was considering Peter Harrington for Hyacinth, but he preferred Miss Leadbetter. Lady Augusta did assure me that she had found someone quite wonderful for Hyacinth."

"One of her circle?"

"The only two remaining men are Mr. Flyte and Sir Francis Cigne. Whilst Mr. Flyte is a good, steady, chap, I fear Hyacinth would consider him too old." Reverend Browning paused. "As for Sir Francis Cigne, I would wish my daughter dead rather than married to him. The man is an unmitigated bounder."

"It has been my experience," observed Holmes, "that women tend to prefer the bounders over the better, more steady, men."

"It is human nature, Mr. Holmes," replied Reverend Browning. "I suspect my own daughter is chasing after Sir Francis. If I could prove it, I would forbid her to visit the manor, regardless of Lady Augusta's reaction."

"We had heard there was some scandal in London involving Sir Francis," I said.

"Not just in London." Reverend Browning paused again, then sighed deeply. "It is not my story to tell, but if you wish to know more, I suggest you raise the issue with the publican of the Wight and Barrow, Mr. Wright. Carefully. As to my daughter's membership, naturally she was invited to join as soon as the society was formed."

Holmes carefully set his cup and saucer down on a small table beside his chair and rose to his feet. I followed suit.

Reverend Browning also rose from his chair. Holmes reached for his hand to shake it. "Thank you for your time, Reverend. You have been most helpful."

"Please feel free to call again, Mr. Holmes, Doctor Watson. I will be pleased to assist you in any way I can."

"We shall do that, Reverend Browning," Holmes assured him. "Once again, thank you."

We took our leave from the vicar and strolled out of the manse into the late afternoon sunshine. A soft breeze was blowing, bringing the sound of joyous birdsong from nearby woods. We strolled across the green, back towards the pub.

"Are you going to ask Mr. Wright about Sir Francis Cigne?" I asked.

Holmes was quiet for a moment, then shook his head. "Not just yet. I think I will wait until I hear from Mycroft." He stopped speaking, and we entered the pub in silence.

Holmes did not speak again, until we were seated in the pleasant dining room consuming a fine dinner of sirloin of beef, with roasted broccoli and potatoes, accompanied by gravy, and bread and butter. His comments were restricted to compliments on the excellence of the fare until we settled to a tasty pudding of damson pie with clotted cream. Scraping the last of the cream from his dish, Holmes looked across at me and said "I think tomorrow would be an excellent time to visit the Prince's Barrow, do you not agree? We cannot do much until Inspector

Crawford returns with the reports I wish to read, so a visit to the scene of the crime, if indeed it was a crime, may prove useful."

I dabbed at my lips with my napkin, before nodding my agreement. "The exercise will do us good, at any rate."

"Spoken like a true doctor."

We thanked Mrs. Wright for the sumptuous repast before heading up to our rooms for a nightcap and sleep.

Chapter Eight

The next morning dawned bright and sunny, though a little cool. I suspected that by mid-morning it would become rather hot.

Holmes and I breakfasted upon poached eggs with sausages and kippers, washed down with an excellent coffee, before heading out to walk to the Prince's Barrow.

We walked the road that led to the manor house for most of the way in companionable silence. As we approached, we could see the barrow off to one side of, and slightly further back from, the house. A walking path branched off the road, clearly leading to the barrow. We turned onto this path and continued on our way.

Looking across at the house I could see signs of activity. A figure could be seen in the gardens, and I noted a curtain or two twitching. Either a servant diligently at work, or someone was watching us. I suspected the later. As visitors to the village, and also the reason for our visit, must have made us figures of some not inconsiderable interest.

The barrow stood on a slight rise of the land. It appeared to be a continuation of the natural ridge that also formed the foundation for the manor house. Lush with summer grass, it could easily have been mistaken for a hillock, except for the flat stones that formed its front and guarded its entrance. The entrance to the barrow was dark and narrow, and faced due west.

One stone, I noticed, was missing. It lay at the foot of the ridge, propped up at a curious angle. I realized that this must be the stone that Peter Harrington had been found beneath. It had been propped up upon rocks by those who had retrieved the unfortunate man's body. Not the largest of the stones, but certainly one that would have been difficult, if not impossible, for one man to move without assistance.

Holmes walked towards the single stone and began to peruse the ground. "I very much doubt that we will find anything, Watson," he commented. "It has been too long since the body was discovered, and far too many people, not to mention animals, have trampled the area. At least we have not had any more rain to further confuse the situation."

I stood back and watched Holmes go about his inspection. He began with the stone, examining it closely, then casting around the area close to it. I watched as he inspected an area of grass and nodded to himself. Holmes then climbed up to the front of the barrow and began to examine it. He disappeared briefly inside it. Holmes came out after a few minutes and waved to me, beckoning for me to join him.

I climbed up to the barrow, coming to stand beside him as he stood before the entrance. I looked around. The view was very pretty, looking west towards the village, and north towards the manor house and its grounds. To the east and the south were woodlands and copses, with the occasional patch of open fields with smoke, from what were no doubt farmhouses, waving lazily in the air.

"Well, my dear Watson, there is no doubt about it. Peter Harrington was most definitely murdered."

"Really, Holmes?" I had to admit to a sense of shock. I had felt that perhaps Algernon Leadbetter had been making a mountain out of a molehill, most likely to placate his grieving sister Verity.

"No doubt about it, my friend." He gestured inside the barrow. "Look here, you can see where someone has stood waiting. There are marks in the chalk soil of good, solid boots."

"Maybe someone took shelter from the rain."

Holmes snorted. "It is not the sort of place you would make a quick dash for to get out of the elements, Watson. You would be soaked before you reached shelter. Besides which..." He gestured to the floor.

Leaning closer I could see dark brown splashes that leant an air of incongruity to the grubby white of the chalk on which they lay. I recognized those splashes, I had seen their like before. The splashes were dried blood.

"Harrington was hit on the head as he entered the barrow," Holmes said softly. "Then his corpse was dragged down to where it was found and the stone placed on top of him." He frowned. "That is where it gets quite awkward."

"Whatever do you mean, Holmes?" I looked away from the blood-stained floor to my friend.

"One man could not have moved that stone and placed it upon the corpse." He strode out of the barrow to where the stone had stood for millennia. "You can see here where a tool has been used to prise the stone loose. The scratches on the stone that sat against it suggest something made of iron."

"A burglar's jemmy?" I asked.

"Here in the country, Watson, it is much more likely to be a mattock."

I frowned. "Maybe the murderer loosened the stone and allowed it to topple down onto Harrington."

"That, my dear Watson, would result in crush injuries, which Mr. Leadbetter assures me that the corpse did not have. I suspect that the stone was slid gently down the barrow and carefully laid upon Mr. Harrington. And that action, my friend, would take substantially more than one man. You could get away with three, but four is more likely."

"Four murderers? There are FOUR murderers?" I could not conceal my shock at the very idea.

Holmes tilted his hand from side to side. "Perhaps. Perhaps not. All we know for certain is that Peter Harrington did not die a natural death. That at least one person was involved in his death, perhaps more."

He walked down to where the stone from outside the barrow was propped up at the base of the ridge. Pulling out his glass, Holmes began to study the rock closely. He called to me and I hurried down to join him.

"See here, Watson," he pointed to the stone. "Leverage marks, and also scrape marks. This slab was prised out of its position and then slid down the barrow, no doubt scraping against loose pieces of flint until it was laid to rest on top of Peter Harrington."

"Oy! What do you two think you are doing?"

We both swung around, startled. Two rather burly men, carrying farming implements were eyeing us with deep suspicion.

"The master don't like trespassers," the largest of the two snapped out.

"We are not trespassing, I assure you, my good sir," Holmes said softly. "Sir Denby Hardcastle has given us permission to be here. I am Mr. Sherlock Holmes, and this is Doctor John Watson. We are investigating the death of Mr. Peter Harrington, at the behest of the Wiltshire Constabulary."

"Sherlock Holmes, eh?" the man who had spoken snorted. "And I'm the Queen of Sheba!" He made a threatening gesture with the tool he carried. "Clear off, or me an' Jack here will throw you off."

"That is quite enough of that, Bill Stokes." A crisp female voice with the hint of a Highland Scots accent spoke from behind the men. They both started, then swung around.

An older woman stood there, frowning at the two of them. She was dressed in a plain, but good quality, dress of dove grey wool, a simple pearl brooch at her throat, and her faded red hair was drawn back in a tight bun. I noticed two young children, a boy and a girl, clung to her skirts. This, I realised, must be the formidable nanny that Inspector Crawford had spoken of.

"The gentlemen are here with Sir Denby's permission. Lady Augusta told me so. Now get back to your work and leave the gentlemen be."

Both men hung their heads, muttered something, and fairly scuttled away. The lady watched them go, then turned her attention to Holmes and me.

"Mr. Holmes. Doctor Watson. Please forgive Bill and Jack. We have had several rather ghoulish sightseers since poor

Mr. Harrington's demise. Naturally, they are rather protective of Sir Denby and the estate."

"Understandable, dear lady, the estate provides their livelihood, after all," Holmes replied. He glanced at the children who were now peeking at us with some curiosity. "You must be the nanny."

The lady put a hand to her chest. "Where are my manners? I am indeed the nanny. I am Moira McDonald."

"A pleasure to meet you, Mrs. McDonald," Holmes said. "Have you been with the family long?"

"Since I was a young lass. I came here at the age of sixteen as a nursemaid to Sir Denby's older brother and sisters, and then to Sir Denby himself. I went from nursemaid to nanny, as is often the case. Families like the Hardcastles prefer familiar faces around them." She smiled down at the two children, "Though I will no doubt retire back to Scotland when these two have grown." The boy made as if to object. She tapped him gently on the end of the nose with her forefinger, "But that will not be for many years yet, Augustus, so there is no call for you to be greeting."

He gave her a sunny smile, "Yes, nanny."

Mrs. McDonald turned back to us. "We shall continue our walk and let you gentlemen get back to your investigations."

Both of us raised our hats to her, as she swept away with the children skipping along beside her. Both children kept casting curious glances back at us as they left.

Holmes observed their progress for a moment. "Inspector Crawford is quite correct, Watson. That is indeed a formidable woman."

"Very much so," I agreed. "Those two men were quite cowed by her."

"Given their age, they have probably known her since they were younger than Sir Denby's offspring."

"That would give any woman a lifelong advantage," I agreed. I looked around at the large stone, and up at the barrow. "Have we seen everything, do you think, Holmes?"

"We have seen all that remains to be seen. The murder weapon, whatever it may have been, has certainly been removed. I do not think there is much to be gained by remaining here any longer. Back to the village for lunch, I think, and then we can decide upon our next move."

Holmes turned away and began to walk back towards the village. I hastened to catch up with him. We walked in silence through the late morning sunshine. Hoof beats caught our attention, causing us both to pause and swing around. A man was approaching on a fine bay stallion. As he got closer I could see it was that rather louche young man, Sir Francis Cigne. He reined in beside us.

"Good morning, gentlemen," said Sir Francis. "A pleasant day to be out and about. He looked towards the barrow and smirked slightly. "You have been visiting the scene of the so-called crime?"

"Indeed," Holmes replied. "One needs must see for oneself where the crime occurred."

"If it is indeed a crime," Sir Francis replied, his smirk getting somewhat wider.

"Oh a crime has most definitely been committed, Sir Francis. And that crime is murder. A very good day to you, sir."

Holmes turned away from him and walked off, his dismissal of the young man clear in every line of his body. As I turned to follow Holmes, I noted that Sir Francis blinked in confusion, as if not much used to being spoken to in such a fashion. He opened his mouth as if to speak, then, clearly changing his mind, closed his mouth, wheeled his horse around, and galloped off.

"That is a very unpleasant young man, Holmes."

"He is certainly rude and impertinent, and I cannot help but wonder what such a man is doing as a permanent houseguest of Sir Denby and Lady Augusta. I am aware, Watson, before you speak, that he was ejected from London society due to a scandal. But you know as well as I do that there are houses anywhere in the country that would welcome with open arms such a hedonistic young man. A comfortable family manor does not, at first glance, appear to be his natural milieu."

We walked on in silence as I turned Holmes' words over in my mind. Eventually I spoke. "You are correct, Holmes. I cannot see for the life of me where Sir Francis fits into this society."

"He is undoubtedly here for a reason, and we will no doubt discover that reason in due course. Now, perhaps we should pick up our speed a trifle. I do not know about you, but I am feeling the need for lunch."

Laughing, I agreed with him and we lengthened our stride back to the village and Mrs. Wright's excellent cooking.

Chapter Nine

Upon our return to the inn, Holmes spoke with Mr. Wright who dispatched his son to the Leadbetters with a note asking for permission to call upon them.

We were dining upon an excellent cottage pie with cabbage, when the lad returned. He came into the dining room and up to our table. "Begging your pardon, Mr. Holmes, but Mr. Leadbetter said that he and his sister would be pleased for you to call upon them this afternoon." The lad scrunched his face up as he tried to recall the rest of the message. "He said they would expect you at three o'clock to take tea."

Holmes dug his hand into his pocket and extracted a shilling which he handed to the boy. "Thank you. You did a fine job with the message."

The lad, whose name I now remember was Paul, gazed at the shilling in astonishment, as if unable to believe his good fortune. Then he closed his fist around it. He grinned at Holmes. "Thank you, Mr. Holmes." Then he dashed away with his prize.

Holmes chuckled drily. "I should really remember, Watson, that a country lad is less likely to have seen a shilling of his own than a city boy."

"At least you will have a devoted messenger," I replied. "He is a bright lad. As bright as some of your Irregulars."

"That he is, Watson. And out here, he may prove to be far more useful than they would be."

I took another forkful of cottage pie. "How do we get to the Leadbetters' home? I know they live in the area, but not where."

"I am sure we can arrange transport with our good landlord," Holmes said as he finished the last of his lunch. Setting his knife and fork across his plate, he dabbed at his lips with his napkin, and rose to his feet. I followed suit, and then trailed him out of the dining room, stopping to again compliment Mrs. Wright on her cooking. It was just as well that we were getting plenty of exercise here in the country, otherwise we might both have grown excessively stout.

Once in the taproom, Holmes hailed our landlord and explained our requirements.

Mr. Wright scratched at his chin thoughtfully. "I have a trap. Paul can take you there and wait for you. He would only have been doing a spot of cleaning. I've a carter or two coming with deliveries, but they have their own lads to help unload. Would that suit you gentlemen?"

"That would be fine, Mr. Wright," said Holmes. "Let me settle it with you now."

The landlord waved a hand. "I'll just add it to the tally and you can pay me when you leave. I suspect you may need Paul and the trap again."

"That we may, Mr. Wright. Thank you. What time will we need to leave to arrive at the Leadbetter's by three o'clock?"

"I'll have Paul be out front at two thirty. Should only take half an hour at a gentle trot. Which is about as much as that old horse of mine can manage."

"Capital." Holmes clapped Mr. Wright on the shoulder. "We shall be down here then." He turned and headed up the stairs to our rooms, with me following.

"Holmes," I asked once we were inside. "Why are we going to see the Leadbetters? Surely we have little to report."

"I have my reasons, Watson. One is to let Mr. Leadbetter know that he was correct: Peter Harrington was indeed murdered. Another is to obtain a sample of Miss Leadbetter's handwriting."

"Handwriting? What on earth...? Oh!" I remembered the note Holmes had found in Harrington's rooms.

"You think Miss Leadbetter may have written the note?"

"Someone wrote that note. I need to discover who." He turned to look out the window. I took out my notebook, pen and inkwell, and set to writing up my notes on our visit to the barrow. When I got to the appearance of Nanny McDonald, I paused. "Holmes?"

"Hmmm?" came the querying reply.

"What was the nanny doing at the barrow?"

"An interesting question, Watson. I have been wondering that myself. It is possible that the children have their father's fixation on all things prehistoric and the barrow is a favourite walk for them. Or..." Holmes paused, turning back from the window to look at me.

"Or what?" I asked.

"Or that that good lady was more than a little curious about our presence and used taking the children for a walk as an excuse to find out what we know."

"Which at this point in time is very little indeed," I said with a faint sigh.

"That will change, my friend. We have barely started upon the case and we already know one of the most important facts about it."

"And that is?"

Holmes gave me a sombre look. "Peter Harrington was lured to Prince's Barrow and murdered."

Chapter Ten

At half past two we presented ourselves downstairs and Mr. Wright took us out the back where young Paul had a pony and trap waiting for us. We climbed in and Paul expertly guided the little animal out of the yard, and we were on our way.

The Leadbetter siblings lived outside the village of Barrow-upon-Kennet, on a small farm on the road that led towards the village of Avebury.

Avebury sat in the midst of a vast complex of stone circles. Sir John Lubbock, the antiquarian whose books Sir Denby owned, had purchased the land the stones sat upon in 1871 when the circles were threatened with destruction, as Sir Denby had told us. The man was later to be made 1st Baron Avebury in recognition of his service to protect Britain's archaeological heritage. I wondered if we would get a chance to visit. I had heard that they were a magnificent sight, far superior to Stonehenge on the nearby Salisbury plain. Avebury would not, I knew, be of interest to Holmes, unless some puzzling crime had been committed there. But I found the idea of the enormous constructions of our remote ancestors to be both thrilling and chilling. I filled my time with these pleasant thoughts as we trotted through the verdant Wiltshire countryside. Holmes, I noticed was sunk deep into his own thoughts, which I suspected were much less pleasant than mine.

Paul guided the trap up to a charming farmhouse set back from the road, with fields spreading out behind it. I noticed the figures of men in the distance obviously hard at work.

The farmhouse was built of Wiltshire stone and flint, much like most of the other buildings we had seen in the county. Ivy climbed up the walls, and roses twined their way around the door frame.

Algernon Leadbetter was standing in the doorway waiting for us. The lines of tension in his body showed barely restrained impatience. "Come in, gentlemen," he said. "Verity is seeing to tea. You have news for us?"

We climbed down out of the trap. Algernon glanced up at Paul. "Take the trap around the back, lad. Mrs. Jones will give you ginger cake and tea whilst we complete our business."

Paul grinned delightedly at the thought of an unexpected treat, and was whistling softly as he steered the trap away.

We followed Leadbetter into the house. Down the hallway I could see a huge kitchen and hear feminine voices from within. We turned to our left into a comfortable sitting room, with windows that looked out on the road in one direction, and out to a tidy little garden on the other. Hollyhocks in a variety of colours danced in the breeze. It was a charming picture.

"Not the place you expect to find a Member of Parliament living, I expect?" Leadbetter's tone was jovial, but there was an odd note to it that made Holmes' raise his eyebrows slightly.

"You do represent this part of Wiltshire," Holmes said mildly. "I would be surprised if you were not living somewhere like this."

"True. True. I have a small place in London that I use when parliament is sitting, but the country air is better for Verity."

It was now my turn to raise my eyebrows. While I would be the first to admit that I am not the most brilliant of doctors, I had seen no sign that Miss Leadbetter had required the clean air of the country for the benefit of her health, which is what Mr. Leadbetter seemed to be suggesting."

I murmured a response that I hope was appropriate and took a seat in one of the comfortable looking armchairs that Leadbetter insisted we sit on.

Miss Leadbetter arrived followed by a maid pushing a tea trolley. The tea things were placed upon a small table, the maid dismissed, and Miss Leadbetter sat and demurely poured tea for us all. Algernon Leadbetter offered around plates of small sandwiches and slices of the ginger cake he had mentioned outside. We ate and drank for a few minutes, mouthing polite nothings in regard to the weather, as the English are wont to do in uncomfortable social situations.

Holmes carefully set his cup and saucer upon the table beside his chair. The Leadbetters straightened up in their chairs, obviously realizing that this was a sign that Holmes was about to get down to business. I took a further bite of my cake before also setting my tea things aside.

Holmes looked at the Leadbetters, his expression tight, giving his normal hawk-like visage a most severe aspect. "There is no easy way to say this, Mr. Leadbetter, so I pray you forgive me my necessary bluntness. You were quite correct in your suspicions. The death of Mr. Harrington was most definitely murder. He was killed inside the barrow and then his body arranged on the ground below."

Miss Leadbetter placed her hand over her mouth. Her eyes widening in horror and shock.

Mr. Leadbetter looked grey, swallowing several times as he tried to speak. It is one thing to suspect murder, and quite another to have your suspicions confirmed.

"Have you any idea who was responsible?" Mr. Leadbetter asked, finally gaining control of his voice.

"Not yet. But rest assured that we will uncover the culprit."

"And the swan's feather?" Miss Leadbetter asked.

"That, dear lady, I have no notion about as yet. It is possible that it may simply have blown there in the wind."

"Blown there? It was clasped in his hand," Miss Leadbetter objected.

"Forgive me, Miss Leadbetter," I interjected, "but as a doctor I have seen many men in the throes of violent death. The hands clutch convulsively at anything that is close by. Mr. Harrington may have grasped at the feather in his final moments."

Miss Leadbetter looked quickly to Holmes. I tried not to feel annoyed at her automatic dismissal of my words.

Holmes nodded. "It is true what my good friend Doctor Watson says." I felt that Holmes was laying extra stress on the word 'doctor.' "The feather may yet prove to be nothing more than a red herring. However, until we know this for a certainty, we shall not disregard it.

"What will you do now?" Mr. Leadbetter asked, giving his sister a quelling look.

"Inspector Crawford of the Wiltshire Constabulary is working with us. He is currently in Devizes. When he returns I will inform his of our discoveries. We shall need to talk in much more depth to the residents of Barrow Hill Manor."

Both Algernon and Verity Leadbetter looked slightly uneasy at that. I shot a glance at Holmes. His quick eyes had noted the look and I could see him mentally filing it away.

"One more thing, I will require some things from a haberdashery. I would be much obliged, Miss Leadbetter, if you could give me directions to one in Marlborough or Devizes."

Verity Leadbetter looked bewildered at the change of subject, then recovering said, "Certainly Mr. Holmes. There are several excellent haberdashers in Devizes."

"Would you please be so kind as to write down directions to them?" Holmes gave her his most charming smile. "I prefer to keep my mind and my memory focused upon my work."

"Of course. If you will excuse me, I shall do so at once." Verity rose from her seat and moved to a small rosewood writing desk that sat in the corner near one of the windows, where it would garner the best light. She sat down, withdrew a sheet of fine paper, took up her pen and began to write.

Holmes turned his attention back to Algernon Leadbetter, his voice was soft and quiet. "Do not allow your sister to get her hopes up, Mr. Leadbetter. It is one thing for me to know that Mr. Harrington was murdered, and quite another for me to be able to prove it in a manner acceptable to a court of law."

Leadbetter nodded. It was obvious that he thought the request for directions was a ruse to remove his sister from earshot. It was equally obvious that he approved of the tactic. "I understand, Mr. Holmes," he said reassuringly. "Of course we would both like to know why Peter was murdered, but I do realize that it may not be possible. I will endeavour to explain the situation to Verity."

At the rosewood desk, Miss Leadbetter gently blotted the paper she had written on, before carefully folding it and bringing it across to Holmes.

Holmes took it from her with a gentle word of thanks, and tucked it safely inside his waistcoat.

"Thank you both for your time," Holmes said to them. "If you can roust young Paul from the kitchen, we will go back to Barrow-upon-Kennet and continue our investigation."

Miss Leadbetter headed to the kitchen to get Paul, and Mr. Leadbetter escorted us to the front door. We stood bathed in late afternoon sunshine waiting for the trap, which came trotting round the corner of the house, a smiling Paul at the reins. We made polite farewells before climbing up into the trap and settling down, then the pony stepped out briskly, no doubt realizing that it was heading for home and the comfort of the stables.

This time I was sure my thoughts were married to those of Holmes, being, as they were, about the Leadbetter siblings' odd unease at the idea of Holmes learning more about the Barrow Hill Manor occupants. I wondered what it was about the idea that made them both so obviously uncomfortable. The residents and guests at the manor, whilst apparently a trifle eccentric, seemed no more so than any other members of the aristocracy that Holmes and I had previously encountered.

The pleasant tea we had partaken of, combined with the gentle rhythm of the horse's hooves clopping on the road, lulled me into a trance-like state, and I was just starting to slip into slumber when we arrived back at the Wight and Barrel.

Back in our rooms, I sat down in a chair, still drowsing slightly. Holmes disappeared into his bedroom, and reappeared with the note from Peter Harrington's rooms. He stood by the light of the window and compared it with Miss Leadbetter's writing.

"Whomever it was that wrote that note to Harrington, it was not Miss Leadbetter," Holmes said after a few minutes.

"It was not?" I sat up straight in my chair, all thoughts of a nap forgotten.

Holmes walked back from the window and dropped both papers onto my lap. "See for yourself. Miss Leadbetter's hand writing is less flamboyant than that of the Harrington note writer. The letters are also more tightly formed."

I compared both pieces of paper, and while I am no expert, I had to agree with Holmes that the papers were definitely written on by two different people. I sighed and handed the papers back to Holmes. "So where does that leave us now?"

"It has eliminated Miss Leadbetter as the writer of the note."

"That is not much," I replied.

"It is more than we had before. Sometimes proving that someone did not do something is as valuable as proving that they did."

"Perhaps." I was not convinced. To be brutally honest, I was not completely sure that we were going to be able to solve this case. The corpse of Peter Harrington was long buried and the trail was far too cold for even a human bloodhound like Holmes to follow. I thought about the note. If Miss Leadbetter had not written it, why were she and her brother so uneasy when Barrow Hill Manor was mentioned?

"Holmes."

Holmes looked up from where he was carefully folding both notes. "Yes, Watson?"

"The Leadbetters; did they seem a little uncomfortable to you?"

"You mean when I mentioned talking to the residents at the manor? Yes, that was very telling, was it not?"

"I cannot think why."

"Inspector Crawford, you will remember, said that it was his belief that Mr. Leadbetter did not care for Sir Denby Hardcastle. It may be no more than the Member of Parliament for the area not wishing his dislike of the local gentry to become known."

I pondered that for a moment. "You may well be right," I said eventually. "If the dislike became general knowledge it could cost Algernon Leadbetter his seat."

"Members of Parliament have lost their seats over much less," Holmes commented. "And Sir Denby Hardcastle is a genial man who appears to be well-liked, for the most part. As for Miss Leadbetter, we do know she is a member of Lady Augusta's society, perhaps her brother does not approve. Or simply that she knows of her brother's dislike for Sir Denby and does not wish us to know."

Holmes went back into his bedroom to store the papers, then came out and flung himself down into the remaining armchair. "It is too early to be theorizing, in any case. We do not have sufficient information for the task." Holmes frowned. "I would really like more information on Mr. Tobermoray Flyte, Sir Francis, and Mrs. Feuer."

"Mycroft will supply what can be found on Sir Francis," I said.

"True. We can ask the inspector for more detail on the other two when he returns from Devizes."

The sound of a gong echoed up the stairs, summoning us to dinner. We headed downstairs to partake of Mrs. Wright's excellent cooking. I was thankful that we were doing so much walking, otherwise I could see myself getting as portly as Mycroft.

Chapter Eleven

We had partaken of breakfast the next morning, and were considering what our next move should be, when Mrs. Wright knocked on our door. "Inspector Crawford is here, sir. Shall I show him up?"

"If you would be so kind, Mrs. Wright," Holmes replied.

The inspector, when he arrived in our rooms, looked tired. He declined an offer of breakfast, but accepted that of coffee with some alacrity. Crawford handled a bundle of papers to Holmes, then availed himself of the coffee pot. After the first mouthful he said, "Those papers are the coroner's report, with post-mortem report attached, and also the police report."

Holmes handed me the coroner's report and its attachment and took the police report for himself.

I decided to read the post-mortem report first. It made for quick reading. It was much as Algernon Leadbetter had told us back in London. Death had been caused by the fracturing of the skull due to blow to the back of the head with an object both unknown and unidentified.

The coroner's report was even less helpful. It noted that a large stone had been placed on top of the corpse, but could give no reason for it. The coroner had returned a verdict of "death by misadventure." I could not forebear snorting derisively.

Holmes looked up from the police report, eyebrows raised in query.

I waved the coroner's report at him. "The coroner went with 'death by misadventure.' The whole thing reads as if he were reluctant to return any other verdict that could possibly reflect badly on Sir Denby Hardcastle. Much is made of the fact that the 'tragic event' occurred on Sir Denby's estate. The post-mortem report, such as it is, is competent enough, but this…" I waved the report again for emphasis.

"The police report reads in much the same manner," Holmes replied. "One would take it to be a fairy story rather than an official document."

"Devizes is not London, Mr. Holmes," Inspector Crawford said quietly. "Only about seven thousand people live there. It is larger than a village, certainly, but village attitudes remain. One does not upset the gentry unnecessarily."

Holmes' answering snort was more derisive than mine had been. "Not a helpful attitude when a man has been murdered," he replied acidly.

"We see so little murder." The words "unlike London" were not said, but were clearly implied. He paused. "You are quite sure that it is murder?"

Holmes then told him of our discoveries at the Prince's Barrow the previous day. Inspector Crawford was troubled by the bloodstains in the barrow, but accepted Holmes' reconstruction of events. He managed a smile when we spoke of the two estate workers and the nanny."

"Nanny McDonald rules the roost amongst the workers," Crawford commented. "Bill and Jack have known her since they were small boys following their fathers around the estate. She has something of an air of authority about her. That formidable lady even scares me, and I have the weight of the Wiltshire Constabulary behind me. I would not worry about her being at the barrow. My father told me that the barrow was Sir Denby's favourite place to go for walks as a boy. Nanny McDonald used to take him. I suppose she is just doing the same with his children."

"That is possible," Holmes agreed. He sank back down into his chair, a frown creasing his brow.

"What is wrong?" I asked, knowing by the virtue of long exposure to Holmes' moods that something about the case was troubling him.

"We have too many people involved, Watson. Sir Denby and his wife. Sir Francis Cigne. Mr. Tobermoray Flyte and Mrs. Celeste Feuer. The Leadbetter siblings. The nanny. The vicar's daughter. Too many people and not enough information to definitively exclude anyone."

"We can certainly exclude the women," I said.

"From placing the rock over Harrington's body, yes, on that point I do agree," said Holmes. "But I do not exclude them from the murder itself."

I opened my mouth to object, but Holmes held up a hand to still my objections. "Answer me truthfully, Watson? Is a woman not capable of striking a man down from behind in such a fashion?"

I closed my mouth and slowly shook my head. "A woman is perfectly capable of doing exactly that. But not the rest of it. According to the post-mortem report Harrington was only slightly under six feet in height and strongly built. As a dead weight I think he would have been too much for even the heftiest of women to drag out of the barrow."

Holmes sat quietly, appearing to absorb my comments. Finally he nodded. "You may very well be correct, Watson."

"We can probably exclude Mr. Flyte as well," Crawford commented.

"Why so?" Holmes asked.

"I asked around whilst I was in Devizes. I went to the bank he used to work for. According to the assistant manager, Mr. Flyte retired with a bad heart. The strain of hauling a body around would quite possibly kill him."

Holmes looked at me. I understood what he was asking. "Without knowing the exact cause of his heart troubles, I could not comment. But it is certain that lugging a heavy corpse about would not do his heart any favours."

Holmes looked thoughtfully at Crawford. "You have initiative, Inspector," he commented. "What else did you discover whilst waiting for the reports?"

"Not much," Crawford admitted. "Mrs. Feuer is almost unknown in Devizes. She does have an account at one of the haberdashers and has been ordering large amounts of dress stuffs recently. None of the banks would talk to me as to what monies she had without official paperwork, and I had no reason to get that. Speaking of official, I sent your request off to London, Mr. Holmes."

"Excellent. Thank you."

Mrs. Wright tapped upon the door and came in to remove the coffee pot and cups. She paused on her way out, her back to us. "Begging your pardon, gentlemen, but I could not help but overhear you talking about Mrs. Feuer. If you want to know more about the lady, maybe you should talk to the vicar."

"The vicar?" Holmes enquired.

Mrs. Wright turned back towards us and nodded. "Yes. When she first came here, Mrs. Feuer spent a lot of time at the vicarage talking with both the vicar and his wife. If anyone in the village knows anything about her, it will be them."

"Thank you, Mrs. Wright."

"If you want to speak to the vicar, sir, you might wish to go before lunch. This is the day he spends the afternoon riding around the farms visiting the sick."

"Thank you again, Mrs. Wright. We shall do just that."

Inspector Crawford took the tray from Mrs. Wright to carry downstairs for her. We followed them downstairs and after depositing his burden in the kitchen, Crawford joined us outside the pub. We walked briskly across the green to the manse.

The maid we had seen previously opened the door, and escorted us into a small study before going in search of the vicar. Inspector Crawford took a seat whilst Holmes perused the vicar's bookshelves, obviously taking note of his reading tastes. I joined Holmes, noting translations of Greek and Roman writers, as well as the religious tracts one would expect to see on a churchman's bookshelves. Reverend Browning came hurrying in a short while later. "To what do I owe the pleasure of this visit, gentlemen? May I offer you tea?"

"No thank you, vicar. We have only just finished breakfasting," Holmes replied. "We have some questions for you, if you are able to assist us."

Reverend Browning took a seat. "I shall endeavour to do my best to answer your questions."

"We are trying to understand the relationships up at the manor."

"That is a subject that could take months to describe," Browning noted drily. "Do you have a particular relationship in mind?"

Holmes took the remaining chair and leaned against the window frame. Outside was a small flower garden and a small patch of lawn. The cat, Belle, was luxuriating in a patch of morning sunshine. I turned my attention back into the room as Holmes spoke.

"Mrs. Celeste Feuer," Holmes replied. "What precisely is she doing there? The lady occupies an anomalous position at the manor, so far as I can tell. She is not a member of the family nor a paid servant. Neither fish nor fowl, as the saying goes."

Reverend Browning nodded his agreement of Holmes' assessment.

"I understand," Holmes continued, "that when Mrs. Feuer first arrived she spent time visiting yourself and your good lady."

The vicar sighed. "She did. Mrs. Feuer is a very unhappy woman. As you are no doubt aware, she was a childhood friend of Lady Augusta, though of a very different social rank, being a servant's child, though I believe such distinctions do not disturb our American cousins over much."

"How did she come to be married to a German industrialist?" asked Crawford.

"The man who became her husband met her on the boat when she, Lady Augusta, and Lady Augusta's father were coming to England for the wedding to Sir Denby. Lady Augusta's father took on the role of father figure to Celeste, and when Mr. Feuer evinced an interest in the girl, undertook to negotiate a marriage for her. They married just after Sir Denby and Lady Augusta, and went to Germany to live."

"How did Mrs. Feuer end up here?" I asked. I was finding myself curious about the lady.

"Her husband died in an accident in his factory. To call him an industrialist was something of an exaggeration. The man owned a single textile factory. After his death it became apparent that they had been living beyond their means and the factory was badly in debt. By the time everything was sold and the debts paid, there was little left for the widow. When Lady Augusta learned what had happened she sent for her friend. Poor Mrs. Feuer has found it hard to settle down. Barrow-upon-Kennet being so very different from a German town. Someone told her that my wife and I both spoke a little German from a period where I taught English at a school in Hohenstein, in Hesse."

Holmes nodded understandingly. "She came here because she was missing her home."

"Very much so. Though once Lady Augusta's society got underway, we saw less and less of her. Mrs. Feuer hasn't visited for at least three months."

Holmes nodded thoughtfully, and then got to his feet. "Thank you. You have answered my question admirably."

"That is all you wished to know?"

"For the moment," Holmes replied. "We have taken up enough of your time. We shall leave you to get on with your day."

Reverend Browning walked us to the door, as we stood there, his wife came up the hallway, looking faintly disturbed. "Simon, have you seen Hyacinth this morning?"

"No, my dear. Perhaps she went for a morning walk?"

Mrs. Browning frowned. "I sincerely hope not. She knows full well that today is laundry day and she is needed to help Sally and I. That girl has become far too selfish and thoughtless of late. She thinks she is better than us because of the company she keeps." With a swish of her skirts, Mrs. Browning disappeared back up the hallway.

Revered Browning watched her go and then turned back to us with a faint sigh. "My wife is correct. Hyacinth has become somewhat intractable in recent times. But my family worries are not your concern. Have a pleasant day, gentlemen."

We left the manse and began to walk back across the green. I noticed a figure running down the road from the manor. It was a man who appeared to be in some distress. Holmes and Crawford noticed him as well, and we hastened to intercept him.

When we reached him, he almost collapsed into Inspector Crawford's arms. It was Jack, one of the estate workers we had met the previous day. His face was white and he clutched at Inspector Crawford's arms. "Come quick. It's horrible."

"Come where? And what is horrible?" Inspector Crawford asked.

"She's all over blood," Jack choked out. He looked over Crawford's shoulder and squawked. "Don't let him come! Don't let him near!"

I looked back to see the vicar coming towards us, a look of concern on his face. The noise had obviously brought him out. John Wright and his son Paul also joined us, as did several other men I did not recognize.

Crawford shook Jack. "You're not making sense, man. Who is covered in blood? Why should the vicar not come?"

Holmes swore briefly, understanding dawning. "There has been another murder," he said.

"The vicar's missing daughter?" I asked softly.

"I believe so, Watson. Come, we must go." Holmes grabbed Jack's arm somewhat roughly. "Enough bawling. Show us what you found."

Jack nodded. He wiped his face with a grimy piece of cloth that presumably had started life as a neckerchief, then started off back the way he had come, with Holmes, Crawford, and myself following behind. The other men come too, including the vicar, who would not remain behind regardless of Jack's imploring. I noted that John Wright and one of the other men kept close to the vicar.

Jack led us to a field on the edge of the manor nearest the village. As we came around the hedge the marked the boundary of the field we saw a pale blue lump half hidden by the hedge itself. The lump turned out to be a young girl in a blue walking dress. She lay stretched out on her back, arms placed carefully at her sides. A strange, almost bloodless, wound was on her forehead. Beside the left side of her head lay a smooth stone disc, with a small smearing of blood along one edge.

There was a choked off cry of horror from behind us. I swung around. Reverend Browning was staring at the corpse with an expression of shocked horror and disbelief. "Hyacinth! Oh dear god! Hyacinth!" The anguish in his voice forced the pitch up several octaves until it was almost a wail of despair. He crashed to the ground on his knees, swaying to and fro with his hands clapped to his face.

I turned away, feeling vastly uncomfortable at seeing such raw, naked, and painful emotion on display. Holmes shot the vicar a compassionate look, before turning his attention back to the corpse of the poor man's daughter.

Crawford looked around and spotted John Wright, who was hovering uncertainly behind the distraught Reverend Browning. "Get him back to the manse, John. Find someone to stay with him and Mrs. Browning. He should not be here for this."

John Wright nodded his understanding and he and his son got the distressed vicar to his feet and gently led him away.

Holmes and I knelt on each side of the corpse of the poor lass. I examined the wound on her forehead. The skin was broken, but as far as I could tell, the bone was intact. "This is not what killed her, Holmes," I said. "There is not enough blood. This was done post-mortem. Her heart had definitely stopped beating when this wound was made."

"What was the cause of death, I wonder?" Holmes murmured.

Between us, we gently lifted Hyacinth Browning into a semi-seated position. At this angle it was easy to see the cause of the poor girl's death. Her hair was in disarray and coated in blood, showing where a blunt object had been used to stave the back of her skull in. The ground where her head had rested was also slick with clotted blood.

Holmes had his lens out and was examining the death wound. He gave an odd little grunt, almost of satisfaction, and carefully worked a small piece of flint from the girl's hair, which he examined critically through his lens. Holmes hummed to himself and stowed the piece of flint in a pocket of his coat.

"Another one," Crawford muttered, running his hand through his hair in agitation. "And this one cannot be anything except murder. But is it related to Peter Harrington's death?"

"Oh it is most definitely related," Holmes replied.

Our moving the corpse had caused a feather tucked into her hair to flutter loose. Holmes held it up. It was the feather of a swan.

Chapter Twelve

A commotion amongst the men gathered around us heralded the arrival of Sir Denby Hardcastle. He was accompanied by Sir Francis Cigne, and Mr. Tobermoray Flyte.

Tobermoray Flyte looked curious; Sir Francis Cigne merely bored. I wondered why the two men had come. Possibly vulgar curiosity on behalf of the retired banker, but Sir Francis? What I had so far seen of the man had not led me to believe that he was the sort of man who would support his host during unprecedented events such as this.

Sir Denby stood looking down at the girl, an expression of sadness on his face. "My wife will be deeply saddened by this. The poor girl. Does the vicar know?"

"He does," Crawford replied. "He was here. Mr. Wright has taken him home."

"I shall send down a bottle of good wine. He and his wife will need fortifying against this ordeal." He shook his head sadly. "I should never have allowed Augusta to fill the child's head with ideas above her station."

Holmes was carefully examining the strange stone object that lay beside Hyacinth's head.

"What is that thing, Holmes?" I asked.

It was Sir Denby who replied. "It is called a discus, Doctor Watson. Around twenty years ago a teacher in Madgeburg in Saxony-Anhalt, Christian Georg Kohlrausch, revived the ancient Greek sport of discus throwing. It is a fine, healthy, outdoor pursuit. I keep several of them, in different weights, amongst the sporting equipment I have for the servants to use. One cannot have one's footmen getting fat."

"Who would have access to it?" Crawford asked.

Sir Denby shrugged. "The key to the equipment store hangs in the butler's pantry. Everyone knows where it is. Featherstone should be able to tell you to whom he gave it."

"We shall speak with him later," Holmes said, getting to his feet. "Inspector Crawford, have you the authority to take charge of this murder inquiry?"

"My superiors in Devizes handed the Harrington case to me, Mr. Holmes. As far as I can tell, this poor girl's murder is an extension of that case. I will send a message to headquarters once I get back. I think patrols around the village and environs are necessary, and we need men for that."

"My workers will happily do that, Jimmy," Sir Denby said.

Inspector Crawford shook his head. "No, Sir Denby. This is police business and therefore requires an official police presence. Thank you for your offer, however."

The inspector organized men to carefully lift and wrap Hyacinth's body in a length of canvas cloth that Sir Denby had sent someone up to the manor house to fetch. A cart was produced, with driver, so that the inspector could take the body to Devizes for post-mortem examination.

Sir Denby Hardcastle then sent for his coachman, Inspector Crawford's brother, Richard, to take his coach and collect Reverend Browning and his wife and take them into Devizes as well. He also sent money with Richard Crawford in case the couple wished to stay in Devizes until they could bring Hyacinth back for burial. I was struck by the gentleness and kindness of this man. Very much the ancient feudal Lord of the Manor; one who viewed those in his demesne as his responsibility.

We waited until the cart with its sad burden had departed, before Holmes began to cast around the area. There was no sign of the murder weapon, which, I supposed was a bit much to hope for, and being a ploughed field, there was no way of telling what footprints belonged to workers and what, if any, belonged to the murderer. Miss Browning's dainty footprints, however, were a quite different matter.

Holmes crouched down and pointed to the slightly blurred impression of a woman's walking shoes. "She stood here, Watson, unafraid. There is no sign of her running from an assailant, ergo, she knew him and therefore had no reason, she believed, to run. Any footprints left by the murderer will have been destroyed by those of the men who discovered the body. But these drag marks tell us that when he struck her down, he then hauled the body closer to the hedge, most probably to delay discovery."

"That did not work," I commented. "The poor lass was still warm when we got to her."

"Indeed." Holmes got to his feet. "I do not think this wretched field has anything more to tell us. It is time we went up to the manor and had a word with Featherstone."

We walked silently across the field, past the Prince's Barrow, and on up to the manor. This time we went around to the rear entrance. A footman lurking outside the kitchen door told us that the butler was in his pantry, and kindly escorted us to the door.

A grey-faced, shocked, Featherstone let us in and sent the footman to fetch a couple of kitchen chairs. He sank down into his chair and gazed at us glumly. "I truly cannot believe it, gentlemen. Little Hyacinth. Murdered."

"You knew the girl?"

"I have lived all my life here, Mr. Holmes. My father was butler to Sir Denby's grandfather. I started out as a hall boy, became a footman, and eventually became butler to Sir Denby. Indeed, the majority of staff have ties here going back to the building of the manor house in the seventeenth century. Son has followed father into various roles around the estate. In consequence I know, or know of, every person on the manor and in the village. The ties between the village and the manor are strong. Those of the staff who do not live in the manor or on the estate, have cottages down in the village."

Holmes nodded his understanding. "So when each new incumbent of St. Nicholas Church arrived, you got to know them?"

"Of course. There is no chapel in the manor, so we all attend the various services in the village. When the Reverend Browning and his family arrived, Hyacinth was about three or four years old."

Featherstone got up and rummaged in a cupboard beside the table and emerging with a bottle of brandy. Three glasses were produced, and he poured each of us a measure. Neither Holmes nor I touched the ones poured for us. Featherstone knocked his back in one swallow. Seeing that we were not partaking, he picked up one of the glasses and sipped at it. His face was a veritable picture of sorrow.

"Bright and pert, she was," Featherstone continued. "Everyone was taken with the girl." His face crumpled. "Everyone will be devastated. Who could have done such a thing? To pretty little Hyacinth? She was growing into a woman, but she was really still very much a child."

"Inspector Crawford claims the girl was a little simple." I said.

Featherstone considered this for a moment. "Young James is probably right. She certainly had a child's way of looking at the world. She would trust anyone. Hyacinth would have been easy prey for a stranger. A tramp perhaps?"

Holmes shook his head. "This was not the work of a stranger. No. A discus from the manor's sporting equipment was used to mark the body. A tramp would not have had access to it. Of more importance is the question of who would have access."

Featherstone looked up at a hook upon the wall, close to the door, where a large brass key hung. "Anyone in the household, Mr. Holmes. The key is kept on its hook as you can see. Anyone who has leisure time is encouraged to partake in healthy pursuits by Sir Denby. As well as several discuses, there is cricket equipment, jumping ropes, a croquet set, archery equipment, javelins, and tennis rackets. If someone wishes to take such exercise they know they can come and take the key, as long as everything is put back to its place, and the key returned when they have finished."

"So all the servants have access?"

"Not just the servants, Mr. Holmes. The equipment is used by guests of Sir Denby and Lady Augusta as well, for all that Sir Denby claims it's just for the servants. Last Saturday, Sir Denby, Master Augustus, and Sir Francis were competing at archery, whilst Lady Augusta, Miss Elspeth, Mrs. Feuer and Miss Browning played croquet."

"I see. Thank you for your time, Featherstone." Holmes got to his feet. I joined him. We left the butler to his sorrow, and his brandy, and left the manor.

We walked slowly back to the village. Holmes was deep in thought. I could not see where we had anything to work on. When I voiced my doubts, Holmes shook his head. "We have two things, my dear Watson, the manner of death and the feather."

"But how are they connected?" I cried. "I cannot see it!"

"At this precise moment in time, my friend, neither can I. But both pieces of information are connected. We have two deaths caused by a fractured skull and a swan's feather was left upon each body. I am absolutely positive that a swan is not the murderer, therefore the feather means something to the killer. Once we know that, we will know exactly who the killer is."

"It all seems so hopeless," I said with a sigh.

"It is not hopeless, Watson. We will find the killer. He has to be on the manor or in the village. Someone knows something."

"What do we do now?"

"I think it is time we had a talk with our host and his good wife. The vicar intimated that they knew something about

Sir Francis. I would like to know what it is and if it could have some bearing upon these murders."

"You think Sir Francis could be the murderer?"

Holmes shook his head irritably. "I think nothing, Watson. As I have said before this is a strange place for a young man such as Sir Francis to rusticate to. He may no longer be welcome in London society, but what is it that makes him welcome here? Sir Francis is not a man for rural pursuits."

"He rides well," I commented.

"Most gentlemen ride well, Watson. You do not need to dwell deep in the country to ride." With that, Holmes closed down and would speak no more to me. We walked back to the village in silence.

Chapter Thirteen

We entered the pub to find the taproom with few customers. I had expected it to be crowded, with everyone wishing to share the news. Holmes saw my face and smiled briefly. "Whilst in London you would find a pub crowded after such an event, my dear Watson, the people of the village still have their occupations to pursue. Villages do not have the level of layabouts that cities do."

"Very true, Mr. Holmes." Mr. Wright had appeared whilst my friend was speaking. "Mark my words, we'll be busy this evening once the day's work is done. Now, you gentlemen would be wanting lunch?"

"If you please, Mr. Wright. Then we would like, if at all possible, to talk to both you and your good wife."

John Wright looked at us for a long moment, as if weighing up his words. Then he shook himself and said "Right you are, Mr. Holmes. Just go through to the dining room. The missus will bring you your lunch. I'll get Lena to mind the bar while we talk."

We went into the dining room and sat down. I gazed out the window at the garden, without really seeing it. Presently Mrs. Wright brought us mutton chops with carrots and potatoes, along with fresh baked bread and local butter. Neither Holmes nor I were inclined to conversation and gave ourselves up entirely to our meal.

Once we had finished eating, the table was cleared and then Mrs. Wright brought a pot of tea, and she and her husband joined us at the table.

Mr. Wright broke the silence. "What do you wish to speak about, Mr. Holmes?"

"I am curious about two people. They do not quite fit the picture of manor house visitors or residents."

"And those people would be?" asked Mr. Wright.

"Hyacinth Browning and Sir Francis Cigne," Holmes replied.

I noticed the expressions on the Wright's faces tightened at the mention of Sir Francis. They exchanged a look. Mr. Wright's seemed to be asking his wife a question. Mrs. Wright nodded once, sharply, then looked away.

Mr. Wright took a deep breath and turned to us. "Young Hyacinth was an odd child. Head full of dandelion fluff, as I've said to others before today. Wanted to be a princess in a fairy story. Could never accept that she was the daughter of a vicar and, in all likelihood would end up the wife of another vicar." He shook his head. "Lady Augusta encouraged her in her fancies. Going so far as to seek a good husband for the lass."

"Who did she have in mind? We did hear Peter Harrington's name mentioned," I said.

"That was whom Lady Augusta had in mind, I understand, but Harrington thought marriage to a Member of Parliament's sister would be more useful to him than that to a vicar's daughter. As for Hyacinth..." Wright shook his head sadly. "She had a fancy to marry Sir Francis. The hound found it amusing. He would not have married her, even if Lady

Augusta had suggested it." Wright's countenance grew dark with anger.

"Why not?" Holmes asked softly.

"Because the man is an animal. His idea of amusement is seducing innocent young girls. Especially those of a class that he would not be expected to marry under any circumstances. It's a pity someone did not kill him rather than Harrington."

I was startled by the man's anger.

Holmes simply nodded his understanding. "You have a daughter." Holmes' voice held a wealth of understanding at the words that Mr. Wright was not saying.

"Aye. She used to work at the manor." The response was curt.

"Until Sir Francis came to stay." It was a statement not a question.

"As you say." Mr. Wright's tone was flat.

I felt we would get nothing more from the Wrights, indeed, I felt Wright was close to violence. Holmes obvious felt the same for he rose to his feet and I quickly followed.

We quietly left the dining room and headed back to our rooms. I waited until we were inside before bursting out with: "That utter bounder! The man needs a damn good thrashing!"

"Indeed," replied Holmes. "I have met the type before. Not one to force himself upon a woman, but gently courts her, wins her trust, then, having seduced her, scorns her."

"I have changed my mind," I declared.

"That was remarkably quick," commented Holmes.

"The man needs thrashing and then to be hanged from the highest tree on the manor!"

"I am sure our good landlord could be persuaded to supply a stout rope." Holmes pulled a sour face. "It explains why the vicar stated he would wish his daughter dead rather than married to Sir Francis."

"Holmes! You don't think..?" I was aghast.

"Of course not, Watson. You saw how fresh the blood was upon the back of the girl's head and upon the grass beneath. At the time Hyacinth was meeting her death, we were meeting her father in the manse. He cannot have been in two places at once."

The mention of this morning's murder brought the piece of flint back to mind. "Holmes?"

"Yes, Watson?"

"This morning, you picked a piece of flint from Hyacinth's hair. Why?"

Holmes looked at me. "It was close to the wound. It may simply have been caught in her hair as her killer dragged her corpse into the hedge. Or it may not."

"You think it came off the murder weapon?

"It is possible. All we know about the weapon is that it is heavy enough to fracture a human skull. A rock would do that passingly well."

I sat down heavily in a chair. "Where will this end, Holmes?" I was aware that my voice was little more than a pleading whine. "Will there be more deaths?"

Holmes sighed. "That is more than likely. The killer has a taste for it now, and in my experience such men do not stop voluntarily. He has to be caught."

"But will we catch him?" I was aware that my tone had turned imploring. That I was looking to my friend for some crumb of comfort. Death normally does not discommode me greatly, being a doctor, but that poor girl's battered head was haunting my thoughts.

Holmes turned away from me, towards the window. "We will try, Watson. We will most certainly try."

Dinner that night was a subdued affair, and Holmes and I returned to our rooms early. I to read a book that I had brought with me from London; Holmes to stare moodily out of the window. This far from our London home we did not have our normal means of either entertaining ourselves or, in this case, distracting ourselves, from our increasingly dark thoughts. The idea of drinking in the taproom downstairs appealed to neither of us.

The rising sun brought with it Inspector James Crawford. Holmes and I were breakfasting upon fried rabbit with fritters, when the inspector appeared beside our table, looking tired and drawn. This time he joined us for breakfast before we once again retreated to our rooms.

Once inside our rooms Inspector Crawford handed Holmes a carefully sealed missive. I could see that it bore Mycroft's handwriting on the outside. It was obviously the report of the Sir Francis Cigne scandal. Holmes took it, but did not immediately begin to read it as I had thought he would.

"What news on Miss Browning?" he asked.

"The post-mortem was completed yesterday and the inquest will be held tomorrow afternoon."

"Will we be required to attend?" I asked.

Inspector Crawford's lips twitched as he attempted to suppress a smile. "No, Doctor Watson. The coroner has said that the presence of yourself and Mr. Holmes will not be required. I suspect that he does not wish the shortcomings of Mr. Harrington's inquest to be aired in public, as they no doubt would be if you gentlemen were to speak."

His face grew sombre. "I must attend as the police officer who saw the body. I will return to Devizes first thing tomorrow. I will have to take Jack back with me, as he found the body. The funeral for Hyacinth will take place the day after. The vicar of St. John's church will accompany Reverend Browning and his wife back here and take the service. It is too much to expect our poor vicar to lead the funeral service for his own daughter."

"Indeed. I expect most people in the village will attend," said Holmes.

"Not just the village. You can be sure that Sir Denby and Lady Augusta will attend. Though I doubt that Sir Francis will be welcome," said Inspector Crawford.

"Speaking of Sir Francis..." Holmes opened the letter from Mycroft and began to read it. There was silence but for the rustling of paper, before Holmes snorted and handed the letter to me. "Well, that explains the Leadbetter's reaction to our wishing to know more about the manor's residents." Holmes' expression was exceedingly sour.

I scanned Mycroft's neat handwriting quickly. He told a tale of debauchery and seduction that would even have horrified the writers of those ubiquitous Penny Dreadfuls. The wives and daughters of many of London's elite were rumoured to have fallen for his dubious charms. Though Mycroft took pains to emphasize that they were only rumours. The last conquest, however, was substantially more than a mere rumour. It appeared that Sir Francis Cigne's last conquest was Miss Verity Leadbetter. They were caught together in circumstances that left Algernon Leadbetter with no other option than to remove his sister from London society, and London society firmly expressed its disapproval by insisting that Sir Francis remove himself from it as soon as possible.

"Did you read this?" Holmes asked Crawford.

The inspector shook his head. "No, Mr. Holmes. I am not in the habit of reading other people's correspondence. Does it help?"

Holmes waved a hand. "Perhaps yes. Perhaps no. It goes someway to explaining why Sir Francis chose to come here."

Crawford gave him an inquiring look.

"Sir Francis seduced Miss Leadbetter," I explained, as I carefully folded Mycroft's missive.

"Ah. I see. So he is here either because he genuinely loves the girl…"

Holmes snorted his contempt for that observation. Whilst I made no noise, I could not help but agree with his sentiments. Sir Francis Cigne struck me as the type of man who loved only himself.

Inspector Crawford continued, "…in which case he has a motive for killing Harrington, and perhaps Hyacinth if she saw something and was holding out for marriage."

"Inspector Crawford," Holmes shot out, his contempt obvious. "You are reading entirely the wrong type of books! I expect that sort of romantic twaddle from Watson, not from a level-headed police officer."

"You do not agree?"

"I most certainly do not, and neither does my good Watson."

"We have encountered his like in London," I explained. "He is the sort of man who considers that the world owes him everything."

"The sort of man," said Holmes, "whose very disposition does not even allow for the concept of romantic love."

My eyebrows rose at that comment coming from Holmes. He interpreted my look with a swift, tight, smile. "I am not being a hypocrite, my dear Watson, I am aware of the concept of romantic love, and I am also aware that it is not for me. As for Sir Francis…women for him are something to be used and disposed of."

"In other words," I continued, "…the worst type of bounder and cad."

"You gentlemen certainly have more experience with this than I do," the inspector conceded. "London would certainly have more of those sort of men than Devizes. From my understanding certain types of men are drawn to the vice of London the way flies are drawn to honey. Why then do you think he is here?"

Holmes frowned. "His type is self-centred and extremely childish in many ways. I suspect he is here to punish Algernon Leadbetter whom he no doubt blames for his ejection from London society."

"How so?" Crawford's tone was curious.

"By planting himself nearby where his presence is a taunt to the man and a humiliation to the woman." Holmes expression grew hard. "By staying at Barrow Hill House, Sir Francis Cigne has effectively isolated Miss Leadbetter. She cannot visit the manor whilst he is staying there, and the man shows no inclination to leave. This letter explains why Leadbetter was content to let his sister marry a country lawyer. Having being ruined in the eyes of society, no better match would have been forthcoming. Sir Francis Cigne may very well have killed Peter Harrington, but it will not have been for love of Verity Leadbetter. Thwarted desires have resulted in murder far more frequently than love has."

"So you do suspect Sir Francis?" I said.

"As I said before, Watson, I think nothing. It is too early to think. We have two deaths. No murder weapons. No real motives. I am ignoring the preposterous idea of romance being the motive. Romance does not explain the most important fact."

"Which is?" Inspector Crawford asked.

"The stone that was placed upon the corpse of Peter Harrington. When we know who placed it there and why, then we will know who the murderer is."

"Sir Francis Cigne...?" Crawford asked.

"Could not have moved the stone by himself. He had to have had assistance. Pray tell me who here would go out of their way to assist him? A young man of uncertain morals who is disliked in the village and no doubt in the manor as well? A young man who has made free with at least one young lass in the manor's employ?"

Inspector Crawford raised his eyebrows at Holmes' last comment, but did not say anything.

"Put like that…" Inspector Crawford sighed. "What is our next move, Mr. Holmes?"

"We go back to visit the Leadbetters. I think it is time that we had Miss Leadbetter's side of the story." Holmes gave me a look of mildly irritated amusement. "Do not look at me like that, Watson. I will be discrete. Far be it from me to humiliate the young lady further. We have both known men like Sir Francis. It is rarely the woman's fault, but inevitably it is she that pays the price. Shall we go?"

Chapter Fourteen

We mounted Inspector Crawford's trap and the amiable Fred guided us out of the village and towards the Leadbetter farm, under Holmes' direction. It appeared that Inspector Crawford had no knowledge of the Leadbetters' place of residence, or, as it turned out, had ever met them. Such knowledge he had of them, which he had imparted to us earlier, had come second-hand from others. Mostly from his brother Richard and from his superiors in Devizes.

Preparation for luncheon were underway when we arrived at the Leadbetter farm. We apologized for coming unannounced, but Algernon Leadbetter waved off our apologies. "I understand that you would not come here so early without good reason, Mr. Holmes."

We introduced Inspector Crawford then Holmes said "Is there somewhere where we may speak privately with you and your sister, without fear of being overheard?"

Leadbetter gave us an odd look before leading us to the room we had taking tea in before. The maid was despatched to fetch Miss Leadbetter, who arrived slightly out of breath.

Mr. Leadbetter shut the door and turned to us. "My servants know better than to eavesdrop. So tell, me Mr. Holmes, what have you discovered that demands such secrecy?"

Holmes gazed at him solemnly. "I have heard from my brother as to the reason that Sir Francis Cigne was summarily despatched from London society."

Verity Leadbetter caught her breath in something very close to a sob.

Holmes turned to look at her. "Pray forgive me, Miss Leadbetter. I did not mean to cause you distress."

Algernon Leadbetter stood behind his sister, placing a reassuring hand upon her right shoulder. She fumbled in her sleeve, withdrawing a small scrap of silk and lace which, in her haste, she fumbled and dropped to the floor.

Inspector Crawford bent down and retrieved the handkerchief, handing it to Miss Leadbetter with a soft smile and a gentle word.

Miss Leadbetter murmured her thanks and dabbed at her eyes with the cloth.

Algernon Leadbetter looked at Inspector Crawford with some considerable interest, before turning his attention back to my friend. "My sister, Mr. Holmes, was a victim of that vile man's honeyed tongue and vinegar heart. He smiled and whispered such sweet nothings as would turn a more experienced woman's head. What chance did my sister have?"

"Very little," replied Holmes. "Watson and I have met men like him before. Capable of swaying the most experienced of courtesans with their blend of charm and roguery. An innocent woman stands not a chance against such wiles."

Algernon Leadbetter relaxed a little, realizing that we did not hold his sister in contempt. "Sir Francis Cigne's family is also from Wiltshire. They come from trade, not that that is anything to despise, you understand. Our own family was the same. The Leadbetters and the Cignes both traded in fine Wiltshire hams and other small goods. Our great-grandfathers were friends. Our grandfathers fell out over some trifle that I know nothing about. It was around the time that his grandfather obtained a title. Perhaps that was the cause, I do not rightly know. I do know that Sir Francis grew up despising me. Even more so once I become the Member of Parliament for the area. He set out to bring me down, gentlemen, using my sister to do so."

Algernon's hand tightened on his sister's shoulder. "There was a party at the Earl of Musgrave's London home. Sir Francis contrived it so that several of his friends would find him and Verity in a bedroom, with him holding her in such a manner as to leave no doubt as to his intent."

"He dragged me there," Verity whispered. "He said he had something to tell me." She looked up at us, face flushed with embarrassment, and eyes damp with tears. "I thought he was going to propose marriage. Instead he proposed..." Her flush deepened and she looked away.

Inspector Crawford reached out and gently took her hands in his own. "Miss Leadbetter, you have done no wrong. Sir Francis has wronged you greatly, as did the society that labelled you pariah and cast you out. That is something we all agree on."

She looked at Inspector Crawford for a moment, then up at Holmes and myself. Seeing no condemnation in our expressions, indeed, both of us felt compassion towards this young woman who had been so dreadfully treated, Verity essayed a watery smile and gently withdrew her hands from Crawford's grasp. "Thank you, Inspector."

Crawford stood there, looking a little awkward and a little sad.

"So Sir Francis is from a Wiltshire family. What links him to Sir Denby Hardcastle?" Holmes asked.

Algernon Leadbetter's mouth took on a wry twist. "Money, Mr. Holmes. Whilst Lady Augusta brought a substantial dowry into the marriage, Sir Denby's hobbies have made short work of it, according to reports I have heard. That is partly why they live permanently in Wiltshire. Sir Denby has closed their London house – partly to save money, partly because of his deep love for Wiltshire, and partly because he cannot abide London society. The last is a sentiment that I share with him, as you will no doubt appreciate."

He frowned. "I understand from local gossip that Sir Francis is paying Sir Denby rather a lot of money to allow him to live there, rather than return to his family's somewhat smaller seat near Melksham. Barrow Hill Manor is close enough to Devizes to let him have access to a decent tailor, though not up to London standards, of course. Not to mention the availability of women, though he tends to prey close to where he resides."

"We have already been made aware of that," Holmes said softly.

Leadbetter raised his eyebrows.

"One of the girls who used to work at the manor," I said, not naming the lass. "No doubt there are others."

"No doubt," Leadbetter sighed. "As to why Sir Francis is here, I suspect it is to taunt both Verity and myself. I try to keep Verity from visiting the manor when I know he is there. Which is practically all the time now."

"In truth," the girl said softly, "I no longer desire to visit. The Society of Ancient Virtues is little more than a farce with him as a member. I do miss seeing Sir Denby, whom I have known since I was a child. I became interested in prehistory due to his enthusiasm for the subject. And I miss the children."

"But not Lady Augusta?" Holmes asked shrewdly.

"No, Mr. Holmes. The poor lady is pleasant enough, but voluble on the subject of her society, and, I think, rather frustrated at being trapped in the countryside. She is a creature born to be the centre of attention, I believe. Our quiet rural pursuits bore her."

"Were you aware there has been another murder?" Holmes asked softly.

Algernon and Verity looked at us in shock.

"Who?" Algernon demanded.

"Young Hyacinth Browning, the vicar's daughter," Holmes replied.

Verity Leadbetter put her hand to her throat. "You are sure it is murder, Mr. Holmes?"

"Very much so, Miss Leadbetter. And by the same hand that killed Mr. Harrington."

"How...?" Algernon Leadbetter broke off, unable to form his thoughts into clear and concise words.

"A heavy blow to the back of the head, the same as Mr. Harrington. A swan's feather was also left upon the body. This time tucked into the girl's hair." He looked hard at the Leadbetters. "I shall not rest. Indeed, we shall not rest, until this son of Cain is caught and hanged."

"Your tenacity is well known, Mr. Holmes. I am thankful that you are willing to do this for us," said Mr. Leadbetter.

Holmes shook his head. "Not for you, Mr. Leadbetter. But for Harrington and Hyacinth. They deserve to have their killer caught."

"If anyone can do it, Mr. Holmes, I am sure you can." Miss. Leadbetter smiled encouragingly. "Will you gentlemen stay for lunch?"

"Thank you, Miss Leadbetter," replied Holmes, "but we must decline. We have much still to do."

This was news to me, but knowing Holmes as I did, I suspected that having got from the Leadbetters what he had come for, he had no inclination to linger. I saw that Inspector Crawford was slightly put out. He certainly would not have minded staying longer in Miss Leadbetter's company, if not her brother's.

We were about half way back to the village when a figure on horseback was spotted riding towards us at great speed. Fred pulled the pony and trap to a halt, and we waited as the figure grew closer.

Inspector James gave a shout as he recognized the figure. "Harry!"

The man, Harry, reined the horse in and looked at us with some relief. "Thank God, I've found you, Jimmy. And the gents from London."

Holmes looked at him, taking in the man's demeanour, and demanded "What has happened?"

"There's been another murder. This one…" Harry broke off, a bilious look crossing his face. "Sir Denby sent me for you. All of you. The master's badly shaken. The mistress is hysterical. And rightly so, I reckon."

"Head back to the manor," Holmes said. "We will be following close behind."

Harry nodded, turned his horse, and galloped back the way he had come. Fred chucked the reins and we began to move off after him.

Inspector Crawford swore softly. "I forgot to ask who has been killed."

"No matter, Inspector," Holmes said softly. "We shall find that out for ourselves soon enough."

"Who is that man?" I asked. "The one who brought the message."

"That's Harry," Inspector Crawford replied. "We grew up together. He started out as a stable lad with my brother. Now Dick is Sir Denby's coachman and Harry is the head stableman, responsible for Sir Denby's riding hacks and hunters."

"Sir Denby keeps a good stable," I commented. "We met Sir Francis out riding a lively stallion the other day."

"Sir Denby is renowned in these parts for the quality of his stable, even though he himself does not ride much. He does not even hunt."

"Unusual in a country gentleman," Holmes observed.

"Sir Denby rides to get him to his precious barrows. After that he would prefer to grub about in the dirt for old lumps of rock." It was our driver, Fred, who spoke. "He's a rum one, that Sir Denby."

"I take it that you are from this area as well?" Holmes asked.

"Yes, sir. Born and raised in Marlborough."

"Few people wish to come from London to Wiltshire to live," Inspector Crawford commented. "More people wish to leave the country to live in the city than the other way around."

"Indeed." Holmes lapsed into silence, and in silence we remained until the trap was trotting up to the front door of the manor.

A footman, whose expression was nearly as bilious as Harry's had been, was waiting for us and led us into the house and up the main stair case. As we hastened along the corridor I could smell what I took to be burnt paper or leaves, overlaid with the smell of roasting pork. I was momentarily puzzled as to the source of the scent, as we were a good way distant from the kitchens. My puzzlement vanished when we reached the end of the corridor where a white-faced footman stood outside a door. He quickly got out of our way and we entered the room.

We stopped dead inside the door, and stared in growing horror.

Mrs. Celeste Feuer sat in a chair beside a bed, her body blackened with soot, and red with vicious burns. Her fire-ravaged silk morning dress and linen petticoats were obviously the source of the burned paper smell. The source of the meaty smell was also horribly obvious.

I swallowed the rising bile in my throat and stepped to the right side of the chair. Holmes walked to the left side of the chair.

I placed my fingers at the pulse point of the lady's throat. "Dead," I said flatly.

"But not from the fire," Holmes replied.

He was carefully examining the back of the lady's head, and he pointed to a spot at the back of her skull. I bent to look and then looked up at both Holmes and Crawford. "She has been struck heavily with a blunt object. The same as Miss Browning."

"And Mr. Harrington," Crawford commented. He sighed. "I'll speak to the stablemen and arrange to take the corpse to Devizes. My superiors are not going to be happy. Hell! I'm not happy!" He sketched us a short bow and then left.

"If he were happy," I muttered to Holmes, "then I would wonder at his sanity!"

Holmes merely grunted in reply.

My friend was carefully examining the remains of Mrs. Feuer's clothing. He rubbed a piece of partially burned linen between his fingertips. "Oil." He handed the cloth to me. "The poor lady's corpse was drenched with paraffin oil to encourage the fire to take more quickly."

I sniffed at the greasy cloth. The odour of paraffin oil was faint; the smell of the burned cloth itself, and that of the lady's body fat, had overwhelmed it. I handed the piece of cloth back to Holmes, who folded it carefully into his handkerchief and tucked it into his pocket.

I looked down at the floor, and made a startled noise.

"What is it, Watson?"

I bent down and picked a swan's feather up from the floor beneath Mrs. Feuer's chair. I handed it to Holmes in silence. He looked at it for a moment, then saying nothing, tucked it into his pocket with the piece of cloth.

We left the room, Holmes instructed the footman to lock and bar the door until Inspector Crawford came to remove the corpse.

Featherstone was waiting at the top of the stairs, and took us straight to where Sir Denby was waiting in his study. My heart went out to the man. He was white-faced and shaken, sitting in a chair staring at nothing, a decanter of whisky sitting on the table beside him, a glass clutched tightly in his hand.

He looked up when we came in and gestured to the whisky. "Help yourselves gentlemen. I suspect you need it as much as I do."

I poured medicinal whisky for Holmes and myself, and topped up Sir Denby's glass. He gave me a somewhat distracted smile of thanks.

He gulped a mouthful of the liquor. "This is dreadful, gentlemen. Peter and poor little Hyacinth were killed on my estate, but this... this...fiend... has come into my very house to hunt."

Sir Denby took another swallow of whisky. "When you first came, Mr. Holmes, I thought you were wrong. That Peter's death was an accident. But Hyacinth's death was no accident, and neither was this. Why is this happening?" Sir Denby's voice was anguished.

"We do not as yet know, Sir Denby. But rest assured that we will find the person responsible for these murders and he will face justice."

"Justice," Sir Denby's tone was bitter. Is there any real justice in this world anymore? I do wonder."

"He will get such justice as the law allows him," Holmes replied, placing his glass on the table, the whisky barely touched.

"Does your wife know about Mrs. Feuer?" I asked.

Sir Denby nodded. "Yes. She was the one who found her. When Celeste did not join us for lunch, my dear Augusta went to check on her."

I winced at the thought of Lady Augusta finding the dreadful remains of her friend. "How is your wife? May I offer my assistance?"

"Thank you, Doctor Watson, but no. Nanny McDonald calmed her down and dosed her with something, laudanum I suspect. My wife is sleeping with Sylvia, her personal maid, watching over her. Nanny is comforting and distracting the children. I do wonder what we would do without Nanny McDonald. Such a capable woman."

"She certainly seemed so when we met her at the Prince's Barrow the other day," I replied.

A smile ghosted across Sir Denby's face. "Taking the children for a constitutional, no doubt."

"That appeared to be her purpose," Holmes replied. We both refrained from mentioning the threats from Bill and Jack and our rescue by the redoubtable nanny.

Sir Denby frowned. "I think, under the circumstances, I shall forbid Nanny to take the children up to the barrow. Or, indeed, far from the house. What do you think, Mr. Holmes? Is that a wise course of action?"

"The killer has not struck at children, even though Hyacinth Browning was little more than a child," my friend said. "However, keeping your children close to you would not be a bad thing under the circumstances."

We left Sir Denby to his thoughts, and his alcohol, and allowed Featherstone to escort us to the front door. A cart was drawn up outside and Inspector Crawford was supervising the loading of Mrs. Feuer's carefully wrapped body into it.

The inspector offered us a ride back into the village with him in the trap, but we both declined, neither of us wanting to be part of the sad little cortege.

We watched the cart, followed by the trap, move slowly off down the drive from the manor. It was almost to the gates before Holmes shook himself and said, "Come, my dear Watson. Let us return to the village. We can do nothing else here for the moment."

We walked away from the manor in silence. Neither of us felt a pressing need to fill the air with sound. I knew that Holmes was brooding on this latest murder, and I found myself dwelling on it. "Holmes! Why is this happening?"

"Hush, Watson," my friend said firmly. "Not here. Let us wait until we are safely within our rooms to continue this discussion."

"Safe? How can we be sure that we are safe?" I cried. "If a killer can strike within the confines of a large mansion, what is to prevent him striking at us at the inn?"

Holmes just shook his head and refused to answer.

Chapter Fifteen

Once back in our rooms at the Wight and Barrow, Holmes asked for a late lunch to be served to us. Mrs. Wright brought up a platter of slices of cold roast rabbit, with pickled cabbage, fine fresh bread, a selection of cheeses, and a pot of good strong coffee. I took the heavy tray from her with a word of thanks.

She turned to leave, then hesitated in the doorway, twisting her apron in her hands. "We saw the cart go through. There has been another killing, hasn't there?"

"I am afraid so, dear lady," Holmes replied.

"Who...who was it?"

"Lady Augusta's companion, Mrs. Feuer."

"Poor lady. I'll remember her in my prayers." With that Mrs. Wright left us to our lunch and to our thoughts.

Holmes helped himself to rabbit, a slice of bread and some cheese, then poured us both coffee as I piled my plate high. We ate in silence for some minutes.

"In answer to one of your questions on the road, Watson, I am sure we are safe here because whatever the cause of the murders is, it is firmly centred on the manor, not upon the village."

"Hyacinth Browning..." I began.

"Lived in the village, but spent much more time at the manor than in the manse," Holmes replied. "No, Watson, the reason, or reasons, behind these killings relates to the manor. The killer is there. Of that, I am quite certain."

"But who? And, for God's sake…why?"

"I do not yet know who the killer is. As for why, ask yourself, my dear Watson, what do the victims all have in common?"

"The manor house, as you just said." I replied.

"Apart from that." Holmes tone was mildly irritated.

I gave him a puzzled look.

"Think, man!"

"I cannot, Holmes." I admitted.

"That blasted society of Lady Augusta's. The Society of Ancient Virtues. All those that have been killed were members."

I sat bolt upright in my chair. Ice trickled down my spine as I realized just what that could mean. "Good God, Holmes! That means Miss Leadbetter, Lady Augusta, Sir Francis Cigne, and that banker chappy…"

"Tobermoray Flyte."

"…are all in grave danger," I finished.

"Possibly," Holmes replied. "It is one connection, no more than that. It could simply be that the connection is the obvious one of their attachment to the manor. It is simply one more piece of information to file away for future reference."

I sank back down into my seat. Holmes drank his coffee and stared out of the window. After a moment a thought struck me and I said, "Holmes."

"Yes, Watson?"

"There was about a month between Harrington's murder and that of young Hyacinth. But less than two days between that of Hyacinth and Mrs. Feuer. What has happened to make him kill again so swiftly?"

Holmes' mouth took on a wry twist. "I rather think, old chap, that we may be the cause."

"What?" I stared at Holmes aghast.

"The police wrote off Harrington's death as a peculiar accident. All was quiet. The killer no doubt thought that he had all the time in the world to make his remaining kills, however many that may be. Then, suddenly, the Wiltshire Constabulary send Inspector Crawford to the village, accompanied by a famous detective and his companion from London, with the avowed intention of properly investigating Harrington's death. The killer has realized that he no longer has the luxury of time. He is, my dear Watson, speeding up his timetable. With less time to make his kills, he is sure to make a mistake. And that mistake is what will trap him. I am sure of it."

"I wish I could be as sure of it as you seem to be, Holmes."

"I am not sure of anything," Holmes admitted softly.

The next morning dawned a little overcast, as if the day itself knew what was to come. This was the day of young Hyacinth Browning's funeral.

A little before ten o'clock Mrs. Wright and her daughter Lena walked with us across the green to the church. Other villagers and some people from the estate were also heading in that direction. Looking up the road out of the village, I could see the funeral cortege approaching. A simple hearse carried the plain wooden coffin. An arrangement of purple and white hyacinths, the flower for which the girl had no doubt been named, rested upon it.

Sir Denby's coach was behind the hearse. From it emerged the Reverend Browning and his wife, and a stout, middle-aged man in a cassock, who was obviously the vicar of St. Johns in Devizes.

Several strong village lads, including Paul Wright, gently unloaded the coffin from the hearse and bore it carefully into the church, with the officiating vicar leading the way, and the grieving parents following behind.

Holmes and I slipped into a pew at the rear of the church. We did not wish to draw attention to ourselves, but staying back also allowed us to see who was present, and, just as importantly, who was not.

Mrs. Wright and Lena sat close to Mrs. Browning in the pew behind. Mrs. Wright occasionally laying a gentle hand on Mrs. Browning's shoulder. The bereaved mother drawing some quiet comfort from the landlady's gentle presence.

I recognized Bill and Jack, and also Harry, from the Hardcastle estate. Sir Denby had attended, sitting next to the Reverend Browning in a fine show of support. Lady Augusta was not there, but that was to be expected with the murder of her good friend Mrs. Feuer happening only the day before.

I noticed Nanny McDonald sitting in the pew across from us, with the butler, Featherstone, seated beside her. She barely took her eyes off the front pew, an expression of intense melancholy on her face. I found myself wondering if, at some point in her life, she had lost a child, and was feeling some empathy with Mrs. Browning.

Algernon and Verity Leadbetter slipped into the church just before the service started and sat in the pew next to us.

Neither Sir Francis Cigne nor Tobermoray Flyte had put in an appearance, making me wonder just how welcome Hyacinth Browning had actually been in Lady Augusta's little society, if they could not be bothered to attend her funeral. But perhaps I wronged them. I thought about the possibility that they were too distraught to attend. This was possible in the case of Mr. Flyte; highly unlikely in that of Sir Francis.

The service was poignant and, mercifully, short. Mrs. Wright and Lena hastened back to the pub to assist Mr. Wright with the arrangements for the wake. Holmes and I stood outside in the churchyard watching the internment, then walked slowly across the green to the Wight and Barrel along with the others who were attending the wake.

Once inside the pub, Mrs. Browning was whisked away by the women into the dining room, no doubt to let her cry again in relative peace.

Mr. Wright provided glasses of wine for all, and plates of funeral biscuits were handed around. I knew Mrs. Wright and Lena had been up half of the night baking them. The delicious spicy scent of ginger and the distinctive aroma of caraway seeds had pervaded our rooms for most of the night. Mrs. Wright had taken it upon herself to do this for Mrs. Browning, saying to me at breakfast that the poor woman had much to be worrying about, without worrying about providing for a funeral.

I sipped at my wine. I saw Holmes take a sip and then raise his eyebrows in pleased surprise. Mr. Wright saw and smiled slightly. "I don't get much call for wine here, Mr. Holmes. Sir Denby sent down a number of bottles from his cellar for today."

"He certainly sent down an excellent vintage." Holmes took another appreciative sip.

"Sir Denby don't know much about wine," Mr. Wright said. "Harold would have made the selection. Best thank him."

"Harold?"

"Harold Featherstone."

"Ah! The erstwhile butler. Thank you, Mr. Wright."

"Pleasure, Mr. Holmes." The landlord turned away to pour more wine for the mourners.

Holmes took another sip of his wine and then said softly "Come, Watson, let us pay our respects to the grieving father."

I looked across to where the vicar was in conversation with Sir Denby. "Should we not wait until Sir Denby has finished?"

"Nonsense, Watson. We can, at least, thank Sir Denby personally for this excellent wine."

We threaded our way through the mourners until we reached the two men who stood partially concealed in the shadow of the staircase.

Sir Denby nodded a greeting to us. The vicar gave us a tired, somewhat watery, smile. "Mr. Holmes. Doctor Watson. I thank you both for coming."

"It was the least we could do," Holmes said softly. "Rest assured, Reverend Browning, that I will do my damnedest to find the man who killed your daughter."

"If anyone can," Sir Denby commented, "…then I have no doubt it will be you, Mr. Holmes." He smiled at the vicar. "I will leave you gentlemen to it. Once again, vicar, my sincere condolences to you and your good wife."

"Thank you, Sir Denby. For your support and for the wine."

"It was the least I could do." His words unconsciously echoed Holmes. Sir Denby looked uncomfortable. The half embarrassed, half pleased look that Englishmen get when being thanked for doing a good deed. He nodded once again and swiftly slipped away. I saw him have a brief word with Featherstone before leaving the pub, no doubt with a great deal of relief. Emotions are tricky things to deal with, and we Englishmen have never really developed the knack.

The vicar looked around the pub. "Is there somewhere where we can have a quiet word, gentlemen? There is something I would like to share with you, but I do not feel that I want to do so in a crowd."

Holmes looked at him for a moment and then nodded. "One moment." He went over to Mr. Wright and said a few words to him. I saw the landlord look across at the vicar, a look of deep compassion on his face, then he nodded to Holmes.

Holmes returned and said, "We shall go up to our rooms. I have told Mr. Wright that you, vicar, are somewhat overcome with the grief of it all, and need to get away. He will keep anyone from searching you out until you have told us what you have to tell. Does that suit you?"

"Admirably, Mr. Holmes. Thank you."

Reverend Browning remained silent until we had reached the sanctuary of our hired rooms. He sat in a chair and placed his head in his hands. After a long moment he looked up and sighed. "In truth, gentlemen, I honestly do not know if my thoughts will make sense to you or whether I am seeing connections that do not exist."

Holmes took the other comfortable chair opposite the vicar. I stood behind Holmes' chair, my hand resting upon the back of it.

"Tell us," Holmes said softly.

"Do either of you gentlemen have a classical education?" came the surprising question.

"I learned Latin as part of my medical training," I replied. "But if by classical education you mean understanding the works of Virgil or Homer, then I have no more knowledge than the average man."

"My education included some of the classics," Holmes said, "But I have endeavoured to forget most of it. It serves no purpose in my work."

The vicar nodded. "It was my daughter's murder that made me see it."

Holmes and I exchanged a look.

"See what?" Holmes asked carefully.

"The connection to the myths of the Romans. Or, rather, the myths of the Greeks that the Romans took as their own. I named my daughter Hyacinth after the flower. But in Greek mythology there was another Hyacinth. Or, rather, Hyacinthus. He was a handsome youth beloved of the god Apollo."

"And...?" Holmes' tone was encouraging. There was a small frown on his face as if the vicar's words had some meaning for him, but he could not quite remember why.

"The god of the north wind, Boreas, also loved the boy and was jealous of Apollo. One day, when Hyacinthus was playing with a discus, he blew spitefully, causing the discus to strike the lad on the forehead, killing him instantly. The flower hyacinth is supposed to have grown from his spilled blood."

I drew in my breath sharply, remembering the discus that had been smacked into the girl's forehead after death.

Holmes swore softly. "Harrington's was not the manner of death, but after."

"Holmes?" I queried.

"Sisyphus and his rock. Doomed in the afterlife to roll a huge stone up a hill only to have it roll back down as he reaches the top."

"What about Mrs. Feuer?" I asked. "Surely there could be nothing so gruesome in mythology as her death."

"You would be surprised, my good Watson." He looked at Reverend Browning. "You knew of Mrs. Feuer's murder?"

"Inspector Crawford mentioned it when I saw him in Devizes last night. Semele, do you think?"

"Semele?" I was really getting quite bewildered.

"Semele, Doctor Watson," said Reverend Browning, "...was a beautiful girl whom the god Zeus, as the Greeks knew him, or Jupiter to the Romans, fell in love with, and got with child. The girl's sisters, urged on by the goddess Hera or Juno, encouraged her to ask him to show her his true form. When he did so, his divine light was so strong that the poor girl perished in flames."

"My God!" I was shocked.

"I did say you would be surprised, Watson," said Holmes.

"Where did our killer find these dreadful ideas? Does this mean we are looking for a classically educated man?"

"Not necessarily," Holmes said. "Surely you have come across the works of Thomas Bulfinch? His books on Greek and Roman mythology, Arthurian legend, and Charlemagne were first published thirty or so years ago. I seem to remember we had them in our house when I was a child."

"Perhaps I heard of them in passing, Holmes. But as a very young man I was studying medicine with little time or inclination to delve into fairy tales." A thought struck me. "Though if they were published thirty years ago, would they still be in print?"

"They have never gone out of print," Reverend Browning responded. "Only six years ago all three volumes were gathered together into one work. I have a copy. Or, rather, I had a copy."

"What happened to it?" asked Holmes.

"Hyacinth lent it, without my permission, to Sir Francis Cigne."

"Did she? Well, that is an interesting piece of information. Thank you, Reverend Browning."

Reverend Browning got to his feet. "I had best go downstairs and support my wife. I hope my information has proved useful."

"It is certainly interesting, but as to its utility, that does remain to be seen," Holmes replied.

The vicar inclined his head and left our rooms, shutting the door behind him. I listened to his footsteps fading down the stairs, before walking around and taking the seat he had vacated.

I looked at Holmes, who was now sunk deep into thought. I waited a few minutes but he did not speak.

"It is beginning to look as if the killer is Sir Francis," I said.

Holmes shook his head irritably. "There is not a single shred of evidence against him, Watson."

"But the book..?"

" ... is not evidence. I have read William Ainsworth's novel 'Jack Sheppard,' but that does not make me a criminal."

"Sometimes I fear Scotland Yard would disagree with that statement."

Holmes gave a short bark of humourless laughter. "The reality is, Watson, our puzzle has suddenly become simultaneously both more complex and easier to understand

"That does not make sense, Holmes."

"It does, Watson, of a kind. We now know what the murderer is doing, but we still do not know why he is doing it. Until we know why, we may never catch him. I am afraid that there will be more deaths before the killer is brought to justice. If he ever is."

"You frighten me, Holmes."

"I frighten myself, Watson. This could very well be the case where I fail spectacularly."

"Never! You will find the killer, I am sure of it."

"Your faith in me, Watson, whilst touching, may be misplaced. I am a fallible human, when all is said and done."

"You are also the best chance anyone has of catching this brazen killer. Do not give up, Holmes. I beg of you."

"Good old Watson." He gave me a tired smile. "I will endeavour to justify your faith in me."

We both sank into silence. After a while the silence became oppressive and I felt the need to break it. "Holmes, what did you think of the turnout for the funeral?"

He raised his eyebrows at me. "A reasonable turnout for the murdered daughter of the local clergyman. Was that what you were asking?"

"There were some notable absences."

"One could not expect Lady Augusta to attend when her oldest friend was murdered in her home just the day before."

"I was thinking more of Sir Francis Cigne and Tobermoray Flyte."

"Ahh! Yes! That was indeed interesting. One would think that as the poor girl was a member of their society that they would put in an appearance. Unless, they too, were distraught at Mrs. Feuer's death and unable to attend."

"Do you thank that is likely?"

"In all honesty, Watson, I do not. I have formed no opinion of Mr. Flyte. He seems a blustering man with little harm in him, but appearances can be deceptive, as we both well know. As to Sir Francis..." Holmes paused, carefully gathering his thoughts, "…it seemed to me that Sir. Francis would not have been welcome, either at the church or here afterwards. I distinctly heard his name being muttered when we were downstairs. He may not have wished to attend, but, equally, he may have been told not to attend."

"Not to attend? But who would tell him that?"

"Most likely Sir Denby. He is obviously close to the Reverend and Mrs. Browning. You noted that he sat in the first pew with them?"

"I did. Nanny McDonald obviously felt for them," I added.

"Oh?"

"Her eyes never left them for the entirety of the service."

"Interesting. I was not best placed to observe that redoubtable lady. Well-spotted, Watson."

Though pleased at the praise, I could not forebear from commenting "Surely compassion for the bereaved is not that noteworthy. I am sure others felt the same."

"You did not see others watching them. Did Featherstone? If you could see the nanny clearly, you must also have been able to see the butler."

I thought for a moment. "No. Featherstone barely raised his eyes to look at the coffin, let alone the poor girl's parents. He seemed to be deeply troubled."

"Ah! That is also interesting."

"I fail to see how compassion at a funeral, or lack thereof, could be construed as interesting, Holmes."

"Because, my dear Watson, it gives us a look, no matter how meagre, at the characters involved and how the events are affecting them."

"But are the nanny and the butler involved? And if so, in God's name, how?"

"Time will tell," was all Holmes would say.

Chapter Sixteen

Time and tide wait for no man, as the saying goes, and we found out early the very next day just how impatient time could be.

We were breakfasting in the dining room, enjoying bacon with coddled eggs, when a thunderous banging was heard on the front door of the pub.

Mr. Wright swore a loud oath, before hurrying to the door. Holmes and I exchanged a look, before rising to our feet and venturing out into the taproom, just in time to see the stableman, Harry, almost fall through the door. He looked at my friend, fear tightening his features into a gaunt mask.

"You'd best come to the manor, Mr. Holmes. There's been another."

We did not ask any questions. I hurried upstairs to grab our coats, before coming back to join the knot of men at the door. Mr. Wright had sent Paul for the pub's pony and trap, and we hastened up to the manor house, leaving Harry to ride on toward Devizes, hoping to intercept Inspector Crawford who would, with luck, already be on his way back to Barrow-upon-Kennet.

We sat in silence as the pony trotted briskly up the hill to the manor. We were met at the edge of the estate by Bill. We got down from the trap, sending a disappointed Paul back to his father, then followed Bill to the duck pond that we had seen from the windows of Sir Denby's study mere days ago.

The body of a somewhat corpulent older man lay face down, with his face immersed in the water, but his body on the bank. A mass of white swan feathers were scattered over the corpse, with blobs of some yellowish substance attached to the feathers and to the man's back.

The ducks had made themselves scarce, but several large swans were hissing and flapping their wings in an aggressive warning display. I kept a wary eye on them as Holmes bent over the corpse. I knew of the legend that a swan could break a grown man's leg with a single swipe from a strong wing, and had no desire to experience for myself whether or not it was true.

"Wax," Holmes said.

I looked down at him without comprehension, still keeping an eye on the swans. He plucked up a piece of the yellow material, rubbing it between his long fingers. "Bees wax."

"Bees wax and feathers?" I was bewildered.

"This is another Bulfinch setting, Watson," said Holmes. "This time it is the story of Icarus."

"Icarus?"

"Icarus was the son of Daedalus the inventor," Holmes replied. "They escaped from captivity on Crete by flying with wings made of feathers and wax. Icarus flew too close to the sun and the wax melted. He fell into the sea and drowned."

Holmes' face twisted into a grimace. "I spent most of last night trying to remember what I read of Bulfinch when I was young, with minimal success. I do wish I could get my hands on a copy to properly refresh my memory. I may have to send to Devizes or London for a copy."

Footsteps heralded the arrival of Sir Denby. He took in the scene, his eyes wide with fear, and sighed. "Who is doing this, Mr. Holmes? And why?" He looked down at the pond, not waiting for my friend to answer. "Poor Tobermoray."

"You know who it is without seeing the face?" Holmes asked, his tone quizzical.

"Who else can it be, Mr. Holmes?" Sir Denby replied in a matter of fact manner. "It is not one of my people. He is dressed like a gentleman. And it is certainly not Sir Francis."

I refrained from commenting that whatever else he was, Sir Francis Cigne was most definitely not a gentleman, by any stretch of the imagination.

Holmes nodded. Sir Denby signalled to the men standing nearby to drag the body from where it lay. They hesitated, as wary of the swans as I was. Sir Denby smiled faintly and gently shooed the swans away. It was obvious that they knew him and trusted him. They waddled into the water and swam across the pond.

Before the men could turn the body over, Holmes kneeled down and examined the back of the head. He looked up and gestured for me to take a look.

I examined the man's skull, noting with a frown the nasty open wound on the back of the head. As with the other victims he had been struck with a heavy object, causing an obvious skull fracture, along with some considerable bleeding. Even if the blow had not killed him, being placed face down into water would have completed the job.

Holmes and I carefully turned him over. The body was indeed that of Tobermoray Flyte, just as Sir Denby had said.

A hurried consultation between Holmes, Sir Denby, and Featherstone, who had come puffing out of the house to join his master, resulted in a couple of old horse blankets being fetched from the stable, and the sad remains of Tobermoray Flyte wrapped away from curious eyes.

Two brawny estate workers carefully carried the corpse to the game larder to await Inspector Crawford's arrival. The game larder was built adjacent to the kitchen. With its stone walls and slate floor, combined with the ventilation windows, it would keep poor Tobermoray Flyte from decomposing too badly if Inspector Crawford was later returning to the village than we hoped.

We accepted Sir Denby's offer of refreshment and were soon seated in his study drinking strong coffee.

"This is a bad business, Mr. Holmes," said Sir Denby, after a few minutes of uncomfortable silence. "Have you any idea who is doing this?"

"Not as yet, Sir Denby. As I said to Watson, it must be a local, but beyond that..." Holmes shrugged. "Some crimes are almost impossible to solve due to motive," he added.

Sir Denby raised his eyebrows. "Explain?"

Holmes paused to gather his thoughts. "Every crime has a motive. But not every motive is obvious to those investigating. The man who strikes out at his wife out of jealousy, for example, is easily understood. But one who creates elaborate scenes such as the one we have just seen, is almost impossible to come to grips with. Maybe one day we shall be able to look at a crime and say the reason was such and such, but I suspect that it will prove to be a field for the alienist, not the detective."

"So you have no hope of catching him?" Sir Denby's tone was despondent.

"I did not say that," Holmes replied. "We will catch him. Sooner or later, he will make a mistake. Murderers always do."

"I hope so, Mr. Holmes," Sir Denby said. "I truly hope so."

Holmes put his coffee cup down and rose to his feet. I followed him. We took our leave of Sir Denby and walked away from Barrow Hill Manor and back into the village.

Our walk was conducted in silence. Neither of us were predisposed to conversation after facing our third murder in the space of a week. It was frankly more than I was prepared to cope with, and I rather suspected that Holmes felt the same.

We had not been long back at the pub, shuffling around our rooms in a desultorily manner, when Inspector Crawford arrived.

Mrs. Wright showed him up to our rooms. The inspector's face was grey and weary, looking haggard in the morning light coming through the windows. "Harry met me on the road. Another one!"

Inspector Crawford slumped into a chair, before struggling upright and digging a sheaf of papers from his coat pocket, and waving them at Holmes and myself. "The post-mortem report on Celeste Feuer. I didn't read it. I didn't have time."

Holmes took the papers from Crawford and read the report quickly. "Well! Now this is interesting!"

Crawford and I looked at Holmes. "When did Mrs. Feuer's husband die, do you know?" Holmes asked.

"I do not," Crawford replied. "My brother tells me that she came to Barrow Hill Manor about two or three years ago, so it cannot have been more recent than that."

"Hmmm." Holmes handed the report to me, which I read quickly, until I came to the section that had obviously prompted his question.

"Oh! My!" Inspector Crawford gave me a quizzical look. I read aloud from the report, "The woman's womb was swollen to the approximate size of a grapefruit, and the contents therein predisposed me to diagnose that the deceased was around two to three months pregnant when she was killed."

"Is that why she was killed?" asked Inspector Crawford. "None of this makes any sense, Mr. Holmes." Crawford's voice held a note of complaint, as if my friend were personally responsible for the situation not being clear to him.

"If we were dealing with an ordinary murderer, such as I mentioned to Sir Denby this morning, I would say yes, inspector. But our killer is something quite out of the ordinary." Holmes frowned. "I am unsure whether normal motives could be said to apply to him. Whatever the case, I believe we need to bring this piece of information to the attention of both Sir Denby and Sir Francis."

"Both of them?" Inspector Crawford queried.

"Yes, Inspector. Both of them. Mrs. Feuer was a guest of Lady Augusta's. Even though she was an American, most likely with no understanding of how the class system here works, I suspect she was unlikely to be dallying with any of the servants. Having been mistress of her own home for so long, she would understand that it is not quite the done thing. Therefore the most likely suspects for impending fatherhood are Sir Denby or Sir Francis."

"What about Tobermoray Flyte? Could he have been the father?" I asked.

"Unfortunately, Watson, that gentleman is no longer available to answer questions," Holmes said drily. "I am afraid that is one question we will never know the answer to."

Inspector Crawford sighed. "We had best be getting back up to the manor, then. I would like to have Flyte's corpse taken to the police surgeon as soon as possible." Crawford pulled a sour face. "The man is starting to talk about charging us rent for the morgue drawers. I think he is joking. I hope he is joking."

The three of us went out to join Crawford's driver, Fred, in his trap. As we settled in, the pony began its weary plod up the now well-travelled road the Barrow Hill Manor. All three of us remained sunk in silence.

Despite all Holmes' bold words to both Sir Denby and Inspector Crawford, I knew he was concerned about his ability to catch this killer. This man who fiendishly recreated scenes from mythology for some twisted reason of his own. If we did not catch him, would he stop when he ran out of myths to recreate? Or would he continue until death itself came for him? These were dark thoughts indeed, and I thrust them aside, knowing that I should concentrate on assisting Holmes with catching our killer.

At the manor, a silent Featherstone conducted us back to Sir Denby's study. The man was seated, carefully cleaning one of his prehistoric stone tools with a soft cloth. He looked up at our entrance. "Back again? Come for poor old Tobermoray, I suppose." Sir Denby carefully placed his piece of worked flint and the cloth upon the table next to his chair, and gave us his full attention.

"There is also some news we would like to impart, and get your thoughts on," Holmes replied. He gestured at a chair, "May I?"

"Of course. Where are my manners? Please, gentlemen, be seated. Shall I ring for coffee, or perhaps tea?"

"Nothing, thank you, Sir Denby," Holmes replied.

"Well, what is this news?"

"It is about Mrs. Feuer," Holmes began.

"What about her?" Sir Denby's face held curiosity.

"You are the medical man, Watson. Pray enlighten our host."

I looked sharply at Holmes, then realized that he wished to observe Sir Denby's reaction without being observed in return. I turned my attention to the baronet. "Inspector Crawford brought us the report of the post-mortem examination of Mrs. Feuer." I paused for a moment, decided against using medical terms, and said bluntly, "The lady was pregnant."

"Good Lord!" Sir Denby sat back in his chair, an expression of astonishment on his face. "Pregnant, you say? Who the devil was the father?"

"We were hoping you might be able to tell us that, Sir Denby?" Holmes said, somewhat drily.

"Well, it was not me, gentlemen, I can tell you that. Mrs. Feuer was a pleasant lady, but not greatly endowed with personality. Half the time I forgot she was even in the house." Sir Denby's face took on a rueful expression. "She was eclipsed by my wife in every way. I understand that it had been like that since they were girls together."

Having experienced Lady Augusta's personality first-hand, I understood what Sir Denby was saying. Around his strong-minded wife, any other woman present would simply fade into the background to become no more noticeable than the wallpaper.

"Forgive us, Sir Denby, but we will need to talk to your wife about this," said Inspector Crawford.

Sir Denby frowned. "Not sure I agree with that, Jimmy. Augusta's been through a lot lately. I don't want her suffering anymore."

Holmes cleared his throat. "It has been my experience that women notice changes in other women more swiftly than men do. It is imperative that we speak to your wife. If we can identify the father of the child, we may perhaps be on the track of identifying the killer."

Sir Denby sat in silence, frowning to himself, and absent-mindedly pulling on his lower lip. After a while he looked up at my friend. "I see your point, sir. Very well, then. I will have Featherstone conduct you to Lady Augusta." He got up and went to the bell-pull that hung next to the door, and tugged on it vigorously.

Featherstone entered shortly afterwards. "Escort the gentlemen to Lady Augusta, please, Featherstone."

"Very well, sir," Featherstone murmured.

Sir Denby returned to his chair and picked up his stone and cleaning cloth before seating himself again.

The butler inclined his head graciously and gestured to us to follow him. We took our leave of Sir Denby and hastened after the retreating figure of Featherstone.

We were led back upstairs to a rather opulent sitting room that looked out from the back of the house towards verdant woodlands from which the faint calls of birds could be heard through the open window.

Lady Augusta lay resting upon a chaise lounge upholstered in soft, forest green, velvet. She looked up as Featherstone conducted us into the room. I noted that her eyes were red from weeping and she appeared listless.

"What do you gentlemen want?" The American accent was more pronounced than it had been when we met her before, and her tone was curt.

"A few moments of your time, Lady Augusta, and a few words," replied Holmes.

Lady Augusta gave him a sad look, but said nothing.

"We have news about Mrs. Feuer's death," said Inspector Crawford.

Lady Augusta looked close to fresh tears. "My poor Celeste. Who did this, and why? My sweet Celeste would not hurt a fly. Neither would young Hyacinth."

Holmes reached forward and gently patted Lady Augusta's hand. "I understand your distress, dear lady, and it saddens me that we must add to it."

"Add to it? Whatever do you mean?" The tone was now verging upon bewildered.

Holmes looked at me.

I cleared my throat somewhat self-consciously. "We received the post-mortem report on Mrs. Feuer." Lady Augusta's face was drained of its remaining colour. The very idea of post-mortems can be somewhat distressing to the fair sex.

"I will not burden you with the details," I said hurriedly, "But the doctor found that Mrs. Feuer was..." I paused for breath, decided against being as blunt as I had been with Sir Denby, and continued, "...with child."

Lady Augusta sat bolt upright and stared at me in shock. "With child? Celeste?" Her tone conveyed her utter disbelief at the notion.

"Yes, Lady Augusta," said Inspector Crawford, coming to my rescue. "The signs were quite clear to the examining police surgeon."

Lady Augusta continued to stare at me in disbelief. It was obvious that she had not known of her friend's condition. "I...I...Who?"

"We were hoping that you would be able to tell us, Lady Augusta," said Holmes softly. "With Mrs. Feuer and you being such close friends, we had hoped that you would have some idea as to what had occurred."

Lady Augusta shook her head. "I have been far too preoccupied with my own affairs," she admitted. "Poor Celeste. She was never very outgoing. Always quiet and in the background. I never noticed." She was silent for a moment. "As to the father. It cannot be Sir Francis or my husband. Nor could it be poor dear Toby."

"Toby?" asked Inspector Crawford.

"Mr. Flyte. Surely his heart would not let him..." her voice trailed off, her cheeks going slightly pink.

"Quite," I murmured.

Lady Augusta was silent for a moment, her expression thoughtful. She looked from Holmes to myself, and then to Inspector Crawford before saying "Perhaps it is the vicar? Celeste was often down there visiting."

I blinked in surprise and noticed Crawford do the same. Clearly neither of us had considered the vicar to be a candidate for illegitimate fatherhood. Holmes, however, did not turn a hair at Lady Augusta's suggestion.

"An interesting suggestion, Lady Augusta, and one we shall take care to examine closely," said Holmes.

We rose to take our leave, when Lady Augusta called out to my friend. "Mr. Holmes, am I in danger?"

"What makes you ask that, Lady Augusta?"

"Contrary to what some people think, Mr. Holmes, I am not a fool. These murders are all linked to this manor. They are not the work of some wandering lunatic. The killer is here."

"I believe that to be so," Holmes replied. "I cannot in all honesty say you are definitely in danger, but it is indeed possible."

"What can I do, Mr. Holmes, to protect myself and my children?"

"Be watchful. If you feel at all uneasy send for me at once. It does not matter whether it be day or night. Watson and I will come to you immediately."

Lady Augusta gave us both a look of gratitude. "Thank you, Mr. Holmes. You have set my mind at rest."

We took our leave of Lady Augusta, and Featherstone once again came to escort us. When we were out of earshot of Lady Augusta, Holmes asked where we would find Sir Francis.

"Sir Francis is in the stables, sir. I believe he has just returned from a ride," Featherstone replied.

We thanked him, and Inspector Crawford led us to the stables, being familiar with them from his childhood on the estate.

We found Sir Francis just leaving the stable, swinging his riding crop back and forth as he walked slowly towards the house. His whole demeanour was one of discontent. He stopped when he saw us. "Are you gentlemen looking for me?"

"As it happens, Sir Francis, yes," replied Inspector Crawford. "We need a few moments of your time."

The young man shrugged, "I have all the time in the world. It is not as if this place is a riot of social activity."

"One wonders why you came here, if your preference is for such a riot," Holmes commented.

"I am sure, Mr. Holmes, you know exactly why I am here."

"I know why you left London somewhat precipitously, as for why you are here..." Holmes paused. "That I have yet to discover, but I am sure your reasons for it are interesting."

Sir Francis chuckled darkly. "Oh yes, very interesting indeed. Now, what can I do for you? I assume that you want something from me."

"Just the answers to some questions," Crawford replied.

"Ask away, I am all ears."

I refrained from commenting that that might very well be the case as there was a decided lack of anything between them. Sir Francis must have divined the general gist of my thoughts from my face, because he smirked at me. The desire to give this irritating and caddish young man a thrashing, which had never really gone away, grew even stronger.

Holmes turned an irritated look on me. I took a deep breath and stepped back out of Sir Francis' line of vision, forcing him to focus on Holmes and Inspector Crawford.

"How well did you know Peter Harrington?" Crawford asked.

"Well enough to find him a bore, but not well enough to care about what happened to him," was Sir Francis' sarcastic response.

Holmes raised his eyebrows, "You were not jealous of him?"

"Jealous? Why on earth should I be jealous?" Sir Francis was momentarily bewildered by my friend's question. "Oh! You mean because of the delectable Verity. I would have to care about her to be jealous, gentlemen, and I most assuredly do not. I found it amusing that Harrington was prepared to take my leavings."

Inspector Crawford grew red in the face, clenched his fists, and took a deliberate step towards Sir Francis. Holmes and I grabbed him by the arms and hauled him backwards, Holmes turned a furious glare on the policeman, who had the good grace to look abashed, even as his eyes were shooting daggers at the smirking Sir Francis.

"I am not jealous, but it seems as though the good inspector is," Sir Francis commented, the smirk growing into a vicious grin. "Even disgraced as she is, Verity is well above your station, Crawford. You started life as a stable-brat on this very estate, did you not?"

"Stable-brat or not," I snapped, "Inspector Crawford is more of a gentleman than you are, sir."

"If you two cannot restrain yourselves, I suggest you return to the house and allow me to question Sir Francis." Holmes tone was icy.

I took another deep breath, shook my head, and once again stepped back from the fray. I noticed that Crawford did the same, though he kept shooting angry looks at Sir Francis.

Holmes glared at us once more, before turning his attention back to the smug man in front of him. "If we can move on from Harrington…"

"If you are about to ask about Hyacinth Browning I will save you the trouble. I knew dear Hyacinth. And I mean that in the biblical sense. Rather fitting for a vicar's daughter, don't you think?"

The grin got broader and, for a moment, Sir Francis reminded me of the cat in that strangely whimsical book "Alice's Adventures in Wonderland."

"The stupid little cow honestly thought I was going to marry her." Sir Francis' voice held a note of contempt. "Me? Marry? I wouldn't marry a peeress let alone a vicar's daughter. Why would I bother? I got what I wanted from her. As I get it from all women I set my attentions on."

"You mean you..." I spluttered to a halt.

"I was dipping my wick into sweet little Hyacinth," Sir Francis replied crudely. He grinned widely at my discomfort.

Crawford was glaring at Sir Francis, and Holmes' face set into strong lines of disapproval, his lips a thin, cold line.

"Mrs. Feuer..." Holmes began.

"Ah! Dear Celeste. I rogered that one once too often." He pulled a sour face. "I put a bun in her oven. A damned inconvenience."

Holmes' nostrils flared. I could see the anger at Sir Francis Cigne's attitude burning in him. He swallowed down his rage and spoke softly, "Tobermoray Flyte?"

"Good God, no! Not my type at all!"

"Sir Francis Cigne! Four people have been murdered. I would deem it a great courtesy if you would treat the subject with a great deal more respect than you are currently showing. Has it occurred to you that all four victims have two things in common?" Holmes' tone was colder than the grave.

"And what would those things be?"

"An association with the manor, and membership of the Society of Ancient Virtues."

Sir Francis stared at my friend, his eyes suddenly wide and startled. He looked somewhat more like a chastised schoolboy than a louche rake. His voice dropped to a whisper. "Are you saying that I could be in danger?"

"It is a distinct possibility."

"I must leave. Go home to Melksham."

"No, you will not," Inspector Crawford replied.

"You cannot stop me."

"If you try to leave the manor, Sir Francis, I will take it as an attempt to flee and will arrest you on suspicion of murder. I may have to apologize for it afterwards, but I will have had the satisfaction of banging you up in the watch-house in Devizes for several days."

Sir Francis gaped at him, his mouth opening and closing several times like a stranded fish. His shoulders slumped in misery. It seemed that the good Inspector was the first man to bring home to him the fact that he was not above the law. I suspected that Sir Francis had been wildly indulged by his family as a youth, and it had soured his character, making him believe that the world owed him everything, and he owed it nothing. The sudden idea that someone could actually want to kill him had shocked the man as much as being doused with a bucket of iced water.

I had speculated on the possibility of Sir Francis being the killer, but if he were, what we had just seen was a finer acting performance than any turned in by Henry Irving.

We watched Sir Francis trudge back to the house, all his insouciant cockiness gone. Inspector Crawford went to arrange for the remains of Tobermoray Flyte to be loaded on his trap, and Holmes and I began to walk back to the village. Without asking, I knew that neither of us felt up to riding in the trap with a corpse: the evidence of our failure to catch the murderer.

Chapter Seventeen

Once back at the pub, I settled into one of the chairs, and watched as Holmes stood brooding at the window.

"Did we learn anything useful today, Holmes?" I asked, more to break the silence than anything else.

Holmes turned towards me. "We learned several things. Whether or not they prove to be useful, remains to be seen."

I frowned. I could not remember us learning anything at all.

Holmes sighed, then dropped into the other armchair, sprawling across it, rather than seating himself properly. "For example, Sir Francis was hinting that there was something unsavoury about Tobermoray Flyte. We shall have to find out what it is."

"Is it relevant?" I asked. "After all the man is the latest victim."

"It may have some bearing as to why he is the latest victim," Holmes replied. "I also found it interesting that, when talking with Lady Augusta, she was adamant that neither Sir Francis, nor Sir Denby, could be the father of Mrs. Feuer's child, and then tried to divert my attention to the vicar."

"We had not considered the vicar," I mused.

"With good reason, seeing as by his own admission Sir Francis Cigne was, indeed, the father." Holmes pulled a sour face.

"Should we speak with the vicar about it? I asked.

"To what purpose, Watson? Sir Francis owns to the deed. I see nothing useful to be gained in adding to the Reverend Browning's distress with silly tales."

"But if we knew why Lady Augusta suggested the vicar..."

"Subterfuge, my dear Watson."

"Subterfuge?" I was quite bewildered. "To what end?"

Holmes give me an irritated look, but when he spoke again his tone was bland. "The most interesting thing about Lady Augusta's comments, is that she put Sir Francis before her husband. That should tell you all you need to know."

It took me a long moment before the penny dropped. I gazed at Holmes with some astonishment. "You mean he's...?"

Holmes nodded. "I surmise so."

"With his host's wife? The utter cad!"

"You have made that observation before," Holmes commented drily.

I shook my head. "I have never seen such a man for using and abusing the fair sex as Sir Francis Cigne. Not even when I was in the army."

"Indeed," said Holmes. He frowned. "No matter how we look at the situation, my dear Watson, the nexus of the crimes is at the manor house. That much is obvious."

I could but nod my agreement.

"Holmes," I said, as a thought struck me, "Could the killer be Sir Francis in league with Lady Augusta?" Even though Sir Francis had seemed shaken earlier, I was not yet prepared, at least in my own mind, to abandon him as a possible suspect.

Holmes leaned back in his seat and gave me his undivided attention. "I have been thinking along those lines since our talk with Lady Augusta. Tell me your reasoning," he commanded.

"Well, we know that there has to be more than one person involved, because of the rock left on top of Peter Harrington. Perhaps they coerced some of the estate workers to help them."

"A nice idea, Watson, except for the trifling fact that the estate workers owe their allegiance, if you will, to the Hardcastle family, not outsiders. If such a suggestion were put to them, I assure you that someone would have gone to Featherstone and thence to Sir Denby."

"Does Lady Augusta count as an outsider?" I asked. I was genuinely curious. In my life I had not had much to do with such people as Sir Denby and his family. It was a strange new world for me, and not one that I was sure I cared for.

"The Hardcastle family has been here since the seventeenth century, and the estate workers' families no doubt as long. Loyalty will be owed to Sir Denby, and his children, but not necessarily to his wife. The indoor workers may feel more loyalty to Lady Augusta," Holmes admitted. "But the killers would not be asking parlour maids to help them move large slabs of rock. However, a man like Sir Francis has most likely brought servants with him. A valet at the very least. Quite possibly a footman to run his errands as well. They may very well be loyal enough to him to assist with such a plan."

"So you are fastening on Sir Francis as the killer?"

Holmes shook his head. "Let us just say that he has gained much more of my attention than he did before."

With that pronouncement I had to be content.

Early evening saw another visitor to the pub. Mrs. Wright showed the stableman, Harry, up to our rooms. He stood in the doorway, twisting his greasy cloth cap in his hands, looking uneasy at being here.

Holmes looked at him, then at the landlady. "Mrs. Wright, would you be so kind as to provide a little brandy?"

"For all three of you?" she asked, her tone mildly disapproving. In her world, stablemen did not drink brandy in the company of gentlemen.

"If you please, Mrs. Wright," Holmes replied.

"Right you are, sir."

Holmes seated Harry in his chair. The man sat on the very edge of the seat, still wringing his cap between his hands with an air of nervous misery.

Mrs. Wright returned with a tray on which reposed three glasses of brandy. Holmes took the tray from her placed it upon the table, and then gently ushered her from the room. Holmes then handed a glass to Harry and one to myself, before leaning against the wall surveying our unexpected guest intently.

Holmes swirled the brandy absentmindedly in his glass before taking a sip and asking gently "What brings you here?"

Harry took a fortifying gulp of the brandy and then spluttered a little as the fiery spirit went down his throat.

"I had a word with some of the other lads, and we felt there was something you should know," Harry said, as soon as he was capable of speaking.

"About Mr. Tobermoray Flyte?"

Harry gaped. "How did you know I'd come about him?"

Holmes shrugged. "It is an elementary deduction. Four people have been murdered. No one has come forward with anything about the first three victims."

Holmes took a sip of his brandy and then continued, gently waving the glass for emphasis. "Flyte was killed this morning, and this evening you turn up in our rooms looking nervous. We have properly met only five servants from the manor. It would be remarked upon if Nanny McDonald visited, and Featherstone would be unlikely to be able to get away from his duties." A small smile ghosted across Holmes' lips. "And our first meeting with the erstwhile Bill and Jack was not exactly amicable. Therefore, you, whom we have met briefly, but without any antagonism, are the perfect choice as messenger."

"Blimey, Mr. Holmes, you really are a marvel."

Holmes waved his hand dismissively, "A small trifle of observation, I assure you." His tone was matter of fact, but I could see that my friend was quietly pleased all the same.

"I feel much better about telling you this now," Harry said. "It's about Mr. Flyte, as you said." He paused, looking unsure as to how to continue. "It's a nasty business, Mr. Holmes."

"The murders?" I asked.

"Them too," Harry agreed. "But Mr. Flyte was nasty. He..." Harry went faintly pink in the face.

"Was he taking a leaf from Sir Francis' book and pestering the women of the estate?" I asked.

"No, doctor. Sir Francis ain't a nice man, but he don't force his attentions on women that don't want him. He, what's the word...deduces them."

My lips twitched as I attempted to suppress a smile. "He seduces them, you mean?"

"That's the word!" Harry beamed his thanks at me. The smile switched off. "Mr. Flyte, he didn't ask and he didn't like women."

I looked at him blankly for a moment. Holmes gave an angry snort. "Young men or boys?" he asked Harry bluntly.

"Boys, Mr. Holmes. He had a go at Mr. Featherstone's grandson, Mark, who is the hall boy. The lad's only nine. And then there were a couple of my youngsters in the stable."

I was horrified as I realised what Harry meant. Tobermory Flyte had been a pederast. I suddenly felt sick. "Sir Denby's sons...?"

"He didn't have a go at them, doctor. Mr. Flyte weren't stupid enough to crap in his host's nest."

"Thank you, Harry," Holmes said softly. "I am much obliged to you for this information. You did the right thing coming to me."

Harry carefully put the glass down, got to his feet, nodded to us and left. Once his footsteps on the stairs had died away, I broke the silence.

"This changes things," I commented.

Holmes shook his head. "We have a reason for Flyte to die, and perhaps the estate workers would assist with that one. But the others... No, Watson. We have some information, but not enough. Not nearly enough." With that, Holmes turned towards the window, and gazed out unseeingly into the gathering night.

Chapter Eighteen

The following morning dawned clear and sunny. Holmes and I breakfasted upon sausages and bacon with poached eggs, and a pot of our host's excellent coffee. Neither of us were inclined toward conversation, so the meal was eaten quickly.

Once we had finished breakfast, Holmes and I headed back out to the manor once again. After brooding on Harry's visit the entire previous evening, Holmes had declared that we needed to talk to both Sir Denby and Sir Francis again.

Sir Denby was once again in his study carefully cleaning another one of his hand axes, when Featherstone showed Holmes and me in.

He looked up with something close to annoyance. "You two gentlemen, again?"

"We apologize for the interruption," Holmes said smoothly, "But we have chanced upon some information about the late Tobermoray Flyte that I am unsure if you are aware of. We also wish to speak to Sir Francis again."

"Francis is in his room. He seems a trifle under the weather. Francis usually goes for a ride after breakfast, but this morning he is disinclined to leave the house. Now, what did you gentlemen want from me?"

"There is no polite way to phrase this," Holmes said. "Were you aware that Tobermoray Flyte was a pederast?"

"What?" Sir Denby sat back in this chair, completely aghast at Holmes' question. "Surely not. I would have known."

"Would you, Sir Denby?" asked Holmes. "It has been my experience that the householder is often the very last person to know what is occurring in his household."

"Who did he..?"

"A couple of stable lads and your hall boy, I believe."

Sir Denby got up and rang the bell summoning Featherstone.

Featherstone raised his eyebrows slightly to see his master so perturbed.

"Is what Mr. Holmes tells me, correct?" Sir Denby demanded. "That your grandson was molested by Flyte?"

Featherstone blanched and looked at the floor. He swallowed several times, opened his mouth, shut it again, and settled for giving Sir Denby a quick, sharp, nod.

Sir Denby sank down in his seat. "For God's sake, man! Why did you not tell me?"

"Mr. Flyte was your guest and your friend..."

"Harold Featherstone, I have known you since I was a babe in arms. I played with your sons David and Harry. I would never have accused you of falsehood. Never, do you hear me? Tobermoray Flyte would have been ejected from here, no matter how much my dear wife complained."

Sir Denby paused and looked hard at his butler, his expression becoming gentle and compassionate. "I do hate to think what you, your wife, and the rest of your family have been going through every day." He paused. "Has this being happening for long?"

Featherstone shook his head. "No, sir. Only since the doctor forbade Mr. Flyte to travel far due to his heart."

Sir Denby looked thoughtful. "That was about three months ago. Flyte must have been preying on boys on his frequent trips to Devizes to visit his old friends before that. He looked up at Featherstone. "Go back to your duties. We will talk later."

Featherstone inclined his head respectfully and left the room.

Sir Denby let out a whoosh of air. "Poor man. I really do hate to think what he has been going through. If it had been my sons..." He stopped, his eyes widening in sudden fear.

"He never touched your sons," Holmes said. "We were reliably informed that the late Mr. Flyte did not crap in his host's nest."

Sir Denby smiled faintly. "Ah. It must have been the stableman, Harry, who spoke to you. He always did have a way with words. Harry is Featherstone's second son, though you would not know it from the way he speaks. When we were boys he loved horses so much that my father let him become a stable-lad rather than make him follow his older brother as a house servant. My father always said that a servant that is happy is a loyal one. Harry's older brother, David, is my valet. Thank you for the information, gentlemen. I am much obliged."

It was an obvious, though still polite, dismissal, but Holmes was not to be deterred. "One more, thing, Sir Denby."

"What is it?"

"Why was Tobermoray Flyte living here?"

Sir Denby glared at my friend's impertinence. Then he sighed and looked down at the stone axe in his hands. "I am not a wealthy man, Mr. Holmes. The estate costs a lot of money to run. Flyte was a friend of my father, as well as his banker. He had no family and when he took early retirement due to ill health, my father offered him room and board here for the rest of his life. Flyte paid for it, of course, my father was not as generous a man as he seemed."

"When did Flyte come to live here?" I asked.

Sir Denby frowned in thought. "It must have been about thirteen years ago. Around the time of my marriage. My wife was taken with Flyte from the first. It was she who insisted he stay after my father died. We needed the money, so I was not inclined to ask him to leave. It also did not feel right. To render him homeless at the moment he had become more or less friendless. I wish now that I had."

"Thank you for your candour on the subject," Holmes said softly. It is much appreciated. After we have seen Sir Francis, Sir Denby, I wonder if I might make free with your library?"

Sir Denby shook himself out of his reverie. "Certainly, Mr. Holmes. Featherstone can show you to it after you have spoken with Sir Francis."

Sir Denby got up to ring the bell.

Holmes was looking out of the window, a thoughtful frown on his face. As Sir Denby reached for the bell-pull, Holmes asked "Do you know what Tobermoray Flyte was doing near the duck pond?"

Sir Denby paused, and looked back over his shoulder at my friend. "Flyte was in the habit of taking a walk around the duck pond in the mornings. He was advised by his doctor in Devizes that he needed a little exercise for his heart, but not too much exertion. Hence the ban on his traveling. A gentle stroll around the pond in the morning and again in the evening filled the bill admirably. Is that all, Mr. Holmes?

"Yes, Sir Denby. Thank you."

Summoned once again by the bell, Featherstone returned and escorted us through the house to a large guest bedroom.

The room, unlike its occupant, was an elegant monument to good taste. The furnishings were Queen Anne. A beautiful bed canopied in green silk dominated the room, flanked by two equally beautiful cherry-wood tables. Sir Francis sat in a chair by the window, staring disconsolately out at the woods in the distance. He did not turn his head at our entrance, merely waving his hand in acknowledgement as Featherstone announced our presence.

"Good morning, Sir Francis. I have several questions for you, if you would be so kind as to answer them." Holmes was all cheerful bonhomie.

Sir Francis turned in his chair to look at us. His eyes were haunted. "What do you want to know?"

"Were you aware of Tobermoray Flyte's pederasty?" asked Holmes.

Sir Francis nodded. "Flyte's tastes were obvious to anyone who had eyes."

"You did not think to tell Sir Denby?" I asked.

"Why should I? It was none of my business. Besides, it was only servant boys." Sir Francis' tone was cold and dismissive.

My dislike of this sordid young man was rapidly increasing. Holmes' nostrils flared with anger at Sir Francis' response. I wondered if he was thinking of his bunch of young rogues back in London; the Baker Street Irregulars as he fondly called them.

"Did you bring servants of your own with you?" Holmes asked, his temper firmly back on its leash.

"My valet."

I noted he did not bother to give us his valet's name.

"We may need to speak with him later."

Sir Francis looked vaguely amused. "Looking for gossip about me, Mr. Holmes?"

"That would be completely unnecessary, Sir Francis," Holmes replied blandly. "I know all about you that I need, or indeed care, to know."

Sir Francis looked needled. "What were your other questions? I am feeling the need for my own company at the moment."

"Only one more. Did Hyacinth Browning lend you her father's copy of Thomas Bulfinch's book on mythology?"

"Yes. I was hoping for something far more salacious than it turned out to be. To be honest I was hoping for something more along the lines of the 'Ars Amorata' or 'The Golden Ass.'" Sir Francis' lips twitched into something that resembled his usual smirk. "Bulfinch was something of a prude."

"What did you do with the book?" Holmes asked.

Sir Francis shrugged as if the question were totally without interest to him. "It is around here somewhere. I put it down one day and never saw it again. Maybe Flyte took it to read. All those gods lusting after young boys would have been bread and meat to him. Ganymede and Hyacinthus and the like."

Sir Francis turned pointedly away from us to stare out of the window again. Holmes pulled the bell-rope to bring Featherstone to escort us. Neither of us bothered to bid farewell to Cigne. We shut the door on him and followed Featherstone to the library.

The library at Barrow Hill Manor was quite large and very well lit. Sunlight flooded in through large south facing windows, making the room a pleasant place to sit and drowse, if one were not inclined to read. I sat in a comfortable wing chair beside one of the windows and proceeded to do just that, as Holmes scanned the shelves, obviously looking for something.

I closed my eyes, enjoying the caress of the sun on my face, only to open them abruptly when Holmes banged a book shut on the table. A glance at my fob watch told me I had dozed for nearly an hour. I looked across at Holmes, who was looking pleased with himself.

I stifled a yawn. "You have found something?"

"Yes. Have you quite finished your nap?" Holmes replaced the book on a shelf before he turned to look at me, one eyebrow raised in amused query.

"Yes, thank you. Are you finished?"

"I have. Let us go." Holmes walked towards the library door. I followed him. I glanced at the book he had replaced on the shelf. It was a volume on medieval symbolism. For the life of me I could not grasp what it could be that Holmes had found in the book that could be pertinent to the case. I knew better, however, than to ask. Holmes would tell me in his own time.

We walked back to the village. My thoughts went to Tobermoray Flyte. I was not surprised that Sir Denby had not known of the man's sordid vice. I had seen it in the army. Young soldiers preyed on by older men, with the officers none the wiser as to the dreadful goings on. As we passed the stables, my thoughts turned to Sir Francis Cigne's behaviour. Could he be our merciless killer?

"Holmes…:"

Holmes shot me a look. "You want to know if I believe Sir Francis Cigne is our murderer."

"Really, Holmes! You are too much at times!"

"I have told you before, Watson. You wear your thoughts upon your face as openly as another man would wear a hat upon his head. As we approached the stables you touched your shoulder, as you often do when you are thinking about your military service."

"I was thinking about the abuse of young soldiers," I admitted.

Holmes nodded. "You looked straight at the stall where the stallion is housed that Sir Francis was riding the other day. At that point your face took on a slightly dyspeptic caste, and you flicked your eyes towards the Prince's Barrow and then towards the field were Hyacinth was found. It was obvious that your thoughts had shifted from the remote past to a more recent period."

We walked on in silence for a while before Holmes spoke again. "As for who the murderer may be, I think I know who it is. I need to send to Mycroft for more information. I only hope we have time to get the proof before the killer strikes again."

"You believe he will strike again?"

"It is not a matter of belief, Watson. I know he will strike again. The questions are at which person and when."

Holmes lapsed back into silence and would not say another word. When we got back to the pub, he spoke for a while with Mr. Wright, before disappearing upstairs. I settled myself at the bar with a pint of good local ale. I was feeling the need for a little liquid comfort. The morning had been both trying and distasteful. I wished with my whole heart that the case would be over soon and we would go back to London.

Holmes came back downstairs with a sealed note which he handed to the landlord along with a sovereign. John Wright slipped the coin into his pocket and headed out the door, note in hand.

Holmes turned around and headed back up the stairs. I finished my pint and followed him.

"Sending a letter to Mycroft?" I asked when we were back in our rooms.

Holmes dropped into a chair. "Yes," came the curt response.

"Holmes," I said, taking the other chair. "I truly cannot see any way you can possibly know who the killer is."

"He has left clues, Watson."

"What clues?"

"It all hinges on the swan's feathers and the note," Holmes replied. "It was simplicity itself to put it altogether after my little sojourn in the library today."

"There is nothing simple about it," I grumbled.

"Patience, my good Watson. We will catch him, never fear."

"I thought you said it all hinged on the rock on top of Harrington."

"I did," Holmes admitted. "However, once I read about the feathers, I realized the true place the rock held in the scheme of things."

"You are not going to tell me, are you?"

Holmes quirked an eyebrow. "What do you think?"

I sighed, and dropped the subject.

We had breakfasted the next morning, and were making plans to perhaps visit the Leadbetter's to appraise them of the current situation, when Harry Featherstone, the stable-man was shown into our rooms.

"Good morning, Mr. Holmes, Doctor Watson. I have a note for you. Lady Augusta gave it to me last night and asked me to bring it to you right away."

Holmes raised his eyebrows, but took the note and opened it. He read the contents; the colour draining from his face. He looked at Harry. "You say Lady Augusta gave you the note last night?" His tone was sharp.

Harry took a step back. "Yes, Mr. Holmes?"

"Then pray tell me why did you delay its delivery until this morning?"

Harry shrugged. "It were Sir Denby, Mr. Holmes. He saw the note and asked about it. Naturally I told him. He told me it were too late for me to be riding to the village and disturbing you gentlemen. Told me to wait until morning, which I did."

Holmes threw the note on to the table and grabbed for his coat. "Hurry, Watson. Hurry. Pray we are not too late. I have made a dreadful mistake!"

Holmes fairly flew from the room, in a turn of speed rarely seen from him. I grabbed my coat and followed the flabbergasted Harry out of the door.

As I passed the table I glanced at the note, and froze momentarily. The note begged Holmes to come at once, because the writer feared her life was in danger. It was the handwriting that caught my attention. It was the same as that upon the note found in Harrington's rooms.

Chapter Nineteen

Mr. and Mrs. Wright gaped in astonishment as Holmes and I ran down the stairs, followed by a puzzled Harry.

At the front door of the inn, we ran into Inspector Crawford, newly returned from Devizes. He took in Holmes' urgency of manner and did not ask questions when Holmes demanded we go directly to the manor. He simply climbed back on the trap, and urged Fred to go as fast as the pony could manage.

Holmes dispatched Harry back to the manor at a gallop, to warn his father that we were coming.

Inspector Crawford tried to question my friend, but Holmes shook his head and refused to answer. "Later, inspector. There are more lives at risk at this moment. Explanations will wait."

And with that Inspector Crawford had to be content.

The ride up to Barrow Hill Manor was tense. Holmes was almost quivering with the tension, reminding me, once again, of a blood-hound on the scent.

The trap had barely stopped before he flung himself from it and ran for the front door, myself and Inspector Crawford panting behind him. A startled Featherstone opened the door.

"Where is Lady Augusta?" Holmes demanded. "Quickly! There is no time to waste."

"Lady Augusta is in her bedroom. You cannot go in there." Featherstone was aghast.

From deep inside the house came a shattering crash, followed by a terrible shriek that was filled with horror and fear. Shoving Featherstone aside, the three of us bolted up the stairs towards to source of the sounds. Footsteps behind us told me that Featherstone was following, albeit at a slower pace.

A female figure lurched out of one of the rooms, and slumped into Holmes' arms, wailing hysterically. Holmes bundled her into Inspector Crawford's arms, before pushing his way into the room, stepping over the mess of broken crockery and food on the floor that had obviously been a breakfast tray, and equally obviously had been dropped by the distraught young woman now in Inspector Crawford's reluctant embrace.

Holmes stopped just inside the door and let forth a low groan of distress. I hastened to him, standing slightly behind him and peering over his shoulder. The scene before me was one of ghastly horror.

Lady Augusta lay naked upon her bed, her head facing left as if in quiet repose. The pillows behind her head, however, were soaked with drying blood. A dead swan lay draped obscenely between her thighs; its wings arranged as if embracing her. The swan's neck was twisted at an unnatural angle suggesting that someone had wrung its neck. Not a feat that would have been easy to perform upon a swan.

I stepped past Holmes, moving to the side of the bed, and placing two fingers against her throat. Lady Augusta's skin was as cold as marble. There was no pulse. I looked away from the dreadful scene of murderous humiliation, and towards my friend.

Holmes was staring at the bed, his face expressionless. He turned his eyes towards me. I could see that they were haunted.

Beyond him, I could see Inspector Crawford still holding the hysterical woman. He was doing his best to comfort her. It was, I felt, a somewhat futile activity. The poor lass would be having nightmares about this morning for years to come.

Holmes' voice drew my attention back to him."

"I was wrong, Watson." Holmes voice was hoarse and low. "I thought she would be the last victim. If the killer was who I thought it was, I thought he would take the other out first. At least giving us a chance to save her."

"Sir Denby is the next victim?" I asked.

Holmes ignored my comment and whirled around to face Featherstone. "Where is Sir Denby?" he demanded.

Featherstone lurked in the doorway, his eyes filled with horror. He swallowed hard. "I am not sure," came the whispered response. "I saw him last night taking some things up to Prince's Barrow. I have not seen him this morning."

A younger man, who was standing beside him, said "Sir Denby was not in his room this morning when I went to dress him."

I realized that this must be Featherstone's other son, David, who was Sir Denby's valet.

The commotion had brought people flocking to the hallway. A combination of curiosity and fear marked most faces.

Nanny McDonald pushed forward, taking the still hysterical woman from Inspector Crawford's arms. "Come, away from there, Sylvia." Her voice was both gentle and firm.

At the mention of the name, I realized that this poor lass must be Lady Augusta's personal maid, whose name had been mentioned in passing before. The woman, who was somewhat more than a girl, but clearly still younger than Lady Augusta, was distraught. I did not blame her. The carnage in the room was almost more than I, both an experienced medical man, and a former soldier, could handle.

"Nanny McDonald," I said, "is there laudanum in the house?"

"Of course there is." She handed Sylvia over to the comforting embrace of a large motherly woman that I took to be the housekeeper.

"Give her a small dose. Enough to calm her, but not to send her to sleep. Inspector Crawford will need to talk to her later, but she will injure herself if she continues on in such a fashion."

Both Nanny McDonald and the housekeeper nodded, and the weeping Sylvia was led away.

Inspector Crawford had taken my place at the door and was doing his valiant best not to retch. One of the footman had not been so lucky. I could hear him heaving in another room.

Holmes arranged with Featherstone for the room to be locked and a guard placed outside, then strode away. I called after him, "Where are you going?"

Holmes did not turn around. "To stop Sir Denby."

Stop Sir Denby? Surely he meant to save him? I exchanged a bewildered look with Inspector Crawford then we both hurried after Holmes.

We headed out of the house. I noticed several of the estate workers were following us. Not in a hostile manner, but much like bewildered sheep will follow a bellwether to the slaughter house.

Holmes was striding towards Prince's Barrow. Looking up towards it, I could see the figure of a man moving around in front of it. What appeared to be a cartwheel rested against the facing stones of the barrow. The figure seemed to be intent on fastening a large bundle of cloth to the wheel.

Holmes swore loudly and began to run again. Holmes never ran. To see him do so twice in one day was as strange as it was terrifying.

The figure in front of the barrow finished fixing the cloth to the wheel, nodded to himself with every air of satisfaction. I saw a small spurt of flame, as if the man had struck a match.

Holmes yelled at the man to stop. The figure froze momentarily as he became aware of our approach. He glanced down at us once and then turned back and gave the wheel a sharp shove.

The wheel wobbled for a moment, before beginning to roll down the hill; the bundle tied to it jiggling and flopping erratically with each bounce.

"Crawford!" Holmes yelled. "Stop that wheel! Get him off it."

With a thrill of horror I realized that what I had taken to be a bundle of rags was, in fact, a man.

The inspector veered away and ran towards where the wheel was heading for the duck pond. The wheel hit the water with a splash, sending a plume of water in the air, along with the terrified ducks and belligerent swans, before settling onto the pond, the weight of the bundle causing it to begin to sink rather than float.

Crawford waded into the pond, calling for assistance to drag the wheel out. I noted that several estate workers, including Bill and Jack, went to help him.

I turned my attention back to Prince's Barrow. The figure was now capering delightedly, like a small child that has pulled off a jolly jape. As we got even closer, I realized, to my horror, that the figure was none other than Sir Denby Hardcastle himself.

I turned to Holmes, mouth agape.

"Come, Watson," my friend said softly. "We need to apprehend the murderer."

Chapter Twenty

That, however, proved to be easier said than done. Sir Denby was not amenable to coming with us. He swore and cursed, in language most unbecoming of a gentleman, and began to throw lumps of flint and chalk at us. As he had the high ground, being up upon the hillock the barrow was built on, it was not possible to rush him and bring him down. We simply stood there. For once Holmes was unsure how to proceed. Nor could I think how to bring the madman back to earth.

We could hear murmuring behind us. Sir Denby's servants were muttering in shock and no little horror. No doubt word of Lady Augusta's horrific death had spread amongst them.

There was a rustle of cloth, and I turned to see the men moving to make way for someone. The straight-backed figure of Nanny McDonald came towards us. She walked past us and stood right at the foot of the barrow, looking up at Sir Denby who was now cackling with a laughter that was almost unholy.

Nanny McDonald placed her hands firmly on her hips, tilted her head up, and raised her voice. Her Scots accent becoming more pronounced. "Denby Hardcastle. You come down here right this minute. You are in a great deal of trouble, young man."

Sir Denby stopped laughing and dancing and cursing and peered down at the foot of the barrow. "Nanny?" His voice sounded somehow small and unsure. More like a small boy caught scrumping apples than a grown man who had committed several vile murders.

Inspector Crawford joined us at that moment. He was soaking wet and squelched alarmingly; duckweed and mud clung to his trousers and boots. Looking towards the duck pond, I could see the trap driver, Fred, helping several servants to carefully load a flopping bundle on a blanket.

Crawford spoke softly so that only Holmes and I could hear him. "Sir Francis is alive. He must have a skull of stone to survive the blow he was given. Will you attend to him, doctor? Then I will send him to the hospital in Devizes. He will be safe there, and, with luck, he will recover. At least enough to give evidence at Sir Denby's trial."

I started to turn to go to the patient, when Sir Denby let forth an almighty wail. I swung back around, the hair on my neck standing up at the dreadful sound.

Sir Denby came barrelling down the slope to crumple onto his knees at the feet of Nanny McDonald. He clutched at her skirts, buried his face in them, and began to weep. She placed one hand upon his shoulder at the base of his neck, and ran the other through his hair in a comforting fashion. "Hush now, my wee bairn." Her voice was gentle and soothing. "Come with nanny. I'll give you some medicine and you'll sleep. Things will be different in the morning."

"That they will," muttered Crawford. "He'll be in the lunatic asylum. I can't see them holding him at the watch-house."

Nanny McDonald helped Sir Denby to his feet and she began to lead him away, as docile as a lamb. As they passed us I said softly "You will give him laudanum?"

"Naturally. Otherwise you will not be able to take him to Devizes." Her arm tightened around his shoulder. "My poor bonny lad, I was afraid it would eventually come to this."

The crowd parted to allow Nanny McDonald and Sir Denby to pass through. I followed them, veering off to follow the group carrying Sir Francis. Behind me, I could hear the murmurings of shock and disbelief rising from the servants. Holmes and Crawford followed, both men sunk deep into their own thoughts.

Sir Francis was gently carried to his room in the manor. There I examined him as best I could. The sheer number of the man's injuries was truly appalling. Sir Francis' skull was most likely fractured, and he had two broken ankles, a broken wrist, not to mention possible internal injuries from being bounced around on the wheel. I was not sanguine about his likelihood of surviving the vicious attack.

Inspector Crawford came to join me as I finished my examination. The inspector had cleaned up and was dressed in an odd assortment of clothing, no doubt borrowed from his brother or from other estate workers. He still, however, smelt faintly of duck weed and mud. It would take a very hot bath with plenty of soap to remove that lingering odour.

"Sir Francis was lucky," Crawford commented, looking down at the corpse-like figure on the bed.

"Lucky?" I raised my eyebrows at the comment. "Well, he is lucky to be alive, I will grant you that. But I am unsure if that state will continue."

Crawford ignored my sarcasm. "There are slight scorch marks on the wheel," he said. "As if Sir Denby had tried to set it on fire."

I thought of the flare of flame I had seen. "If Sir Denby had been thinking clearly, then he would have tried to set fire to Sir Francis himself," I said. "Burns alongside everything else would no doubt have finished him off."

Crawford looked at me. "As I said. He was lucky."

I had to own that perhaps the inspector was right.

An hour later saw Sir Francis carefully placed in the Hardcastle's coach, and accompanied by two footmen to watch over him, was dispatched to Devizes Cottage Hospital, with Inspector Crawford's brother at the reins.

Richard Crawford was also carrying a note to Inspector Crawford's superiors, asking for more police officers to escort Sir Denby into Devizes. He would deliver it after they had delivered Sir Francis to the hospital.

I checked on Sir Denby and found him in a deep laudanum-induced sleep. At Inspector Crawford's instructions, his arms and legs had been bound to the bed posts with soft sheets. I winced at the sight. The restraining of lunatics is sometimes necessary, but it was not a sight I cared for. Even the worst of lunatics was a human being, deserving of humane treatment.

Nanny McDonald was not happy and proceeded to let me know it. "Is there truly a need for that barbarity, doctor? Jimmy Crawford insisted on it. The poor lamb is so full of laudanum he will sleep for a week."

It was an exaggeration, I knew. Before I could reply, Crawford spoke from the doorway. "Procedures, Nanny. My superiors will expect Sir Denby to be properly restrained until we can take him in."

Inspector Crawford looked at the man on the bed, his expression sad. "Sir Denby was good to me when I was a child. I never thought I would ever be in this situation." He shook himself. "I am forgetting my message. Mr. Holmes wants you, Doctor Watson. Will you please joins us, Nanny? Mr. Holmes wishes to speak with both you and Featherstone in the study."

Nanny McDonald gave Sir Denby one last look, then nodded, and headed out of the room. We followed her; Inspector Crawford shutting the door behind him, and locking it securely. There were two more footmen waiting in the hallway who took up guarding positions, one each side of the now locked door.

We walked in silence down to the study where Holmes and I had first met Sir Denby. My mind was reeling. I could not believe that the pleasant, thoughtful, caring, man we had met had turned out to be a vicious, and quite obviously insane, killer. I wondered that I had not seen the signs. I then began to wonder how Holmes had missed them.

Holmes lips twisted into a grimace when he saw me. Once again, my thoughts had displayed themselves upon my face. "I made a crucial mistake, Watson," Holmes said softly, from where he was seated. "I saw two men, both fearful, but of what, I could not tell. In the case of Sir Francis, it was fear of death; in that of Sir Denby it was fear of discovery. Fear is easy to recognize, but the cause often eludes. I had thought that perhaps Sir Francis' fear was that of being discovered. In that I was most definitely wrong."

Nanny McDonald sat down next to Featherstone, who appeared to find the floor to be of great interest.

Crawford leaned against one of the bookshelves, and I took the chair beside that of Holmes. All three of us were facing the two servants. We sat in silence for a while, then Nanny McDonald looked at Holmes. "What do you want to know, Mr. Holmes?"

"Did you know? Did any of you know?"

It was Featherstone who answered, simply shaking his head.

Nanny McDonald sighed. "Denby was an unusual child. From a very young age he was fascinated by the Prince's Barrow, and the by relics of the prehistoric past. A quiet, somewhat solitary, boy, who would rather hunt for ancient tools than join his older brother and father in what they considered manly pursuits."

"Such as?" Holmes asked.

"Hunting, for the main. Denby never cared for killing things."

I thought of the five people, possibly six, that Sir Denby had murdered and could not restrain a snort.

Nanny McDonald ignored me and continued, "He changed as he grew up."

"The master began to change when Sir Matthew wanted to send him away," Featherstone said.

"Send him away?" Holmes queried.

"Denby's older brother, Montgomery, was to inherit the title. Sir Matthew decided that Denby lacked the fortitude to join the military, so decided to send him to Oxford to be educated for the church. Denby did not want to go, because it meant leaving Wiltshire," Nanny McDonald explained.

I frowned. "Surely he would have been able to come back? Plenty of churches in Wiltshire."

Holmes shook his head. "My dear Watson, I assure you that would not have been the case. He could hardly have come home and taken over the parish of St. Nicholas. A man of Sir Denby Hardcastle's family standing would not be expected to be the incumbent of a small parish church. No doubt his father would have bought him a benefice in a large church in a city. Probably in Wiltshire, where he had influence, but there would certainly be no barrows for Sir Denby to explore."

"Exactly, Mr. Holmes," said Nanny McDonald. "The poor lad went into a decline. Montgomery chaffed him about it. None too gently either."

"Ah. When exactly did the brother die?"

"About two weeks before Sir Denby was due to leave. Montgomery was found face down in the duck pond after a night's drinking at the Wight and Barrow. Sir Malcolm was distraught," said Featherstone.

Holmes studied the two servants for a moment, before bluntly asking "Did Sir Denby murder his brother?"

I looked at Holmes in shock. The thought had not occurred to me, and from the sound Inspector Crawford made it was obvious that he had not thought of the possibility either. Holmes looked at me. "I sent to Mycroft for information on Montgomery Hardcastle's death. I have not heard back from him, but it is moot now."

Holmes turned a hard-eyed gaze on Featherstone.

Featherstone swallowed convulsively. "We suspected it, Mr. Holmes," he whispered. "But we had no proof. I think Sir Malcolm suspected it as well, because he watched Sir Denby like a hawk after that."

"It is why you stayed on, Mrs. McDonald, isn't it?" asked Holmes. "A grown man has no need of a nanny, but a nurse…?

"It is as you say, Mr. Holmes. Sir Malcolm asked me to remain as I was one of the few people Denby would listen to."

"What possessed Sir Denby to marry Lady Augusta? On the surface it seems an unlikely pairing."

"That was Sir Malcom's doing, Mr. Holmes," Featherstone replied. "I formed the opinion that he wished for a strong woman who could control his son's odder impulses. Of course, the money she brought with her was also useful."

"Indeed. Sir Denby was not happy with his choice of bride," Holmes said softly. It was a clearly statement not a question.

"He was not," Nanny affirmed. "Denby would have preferred to marry some local lass that shared his interests. It was never a happy marriage. Even when the children came along. Oh Denby was proud of young Henry, and pleased with

191

Augustus and Elspeth, but he was a remote figure to them. And even more distant to his wife. Once Elspeth was born, he ceased going to her bed."

My eyebrows shot up at this candid disclosure. Nanny McDonald saw my look. "Lady Augusta confided in me. She was pleased rather than otherwise. It was her opinion that she had done her duty, and she was thankful to be now spared Denby's attentions."

"Most definitely not a happy marriage," Holmes observed.

"No, it was not. But I never would have imagined that it would come to this," Nanny McDonald replied.

"Indeed. As to the murders...I understand his motives, but the matter of the rock on top of Mr. Harrington..."

Featherstone sighed. "That was Bill and Jack. They found the body. They were afraid that Sir Denby had killed Mr. Harrington accidently, so decided to try and make the death look like an accident. A couple of the other workers helped them move a loose rock from the front of the barrow down the slope and place it on top of Mr. Harrington."

Inspector Crawford stirred. "I should really charge them with something. Conspiring to pervert the course of justice comes to mind. If they hadn't interfered then the other murders may not have occurred."

"Did they witness Sir Denby killing Mr. Harrington?" Holmes asked.

"No, Mr. Holmes."

"If that is the case then I fail to see, inspector, how you believe Sir Denby would have been arrested for the first murder.

He left few clues, none of which pointed directly at himself. The footmarks in the barrow could have been made by anyone. The floor of the barrow is the same mixture of chalk and flint that is found all over the estate, and indeed over many parts of Wiltshire. Every single man who works here will have their boots covered in it. I have made a study of different types of soil and what can be learned from them. I shall send you a copy when I return to London. You may derive some small benefit from it."

"Holmes," I said, "I am confused. How did the murders change from a simple one that was covered up to the elaborate charades that came later? Remember what Reverend Browning said about them resembling classical scenes?"

"That, my dear Watson, was the result of Sir Denby deciding to cast blame upon Sir Francis. He no doubt spotted Sir Francis reading the book. There is also a copy in the library here."

"If there is a copy here, why on earth did Sir Francis induced Hyacinth to take her father's copy for him?" Crawford asked.

Holmes shrugged. "I very much doubt Sir Francis spent any time in the library here, and I also suspect that the book was an excuse to spend time alone with Miss Browning. The first steps on his path to her seduction."

I pursed my lips in disapproval.

"About Miss Browning's death," Featherstone began, "Sir Denby had his own key to the room where the sporting equipment was stored. He said he didn't want to be distracting people downstairs from their work by coming to get the key."

Crawford gave him a cold look. "Did it not occur to you to tell us this at the time of Hyacinth's murder? Your inaction may very well have caused Mrs. Feuer and Mr. Flyte's deaths."

Featherstone looked back at the ground, shoulders slumped in a picture of sheer dejection.

"Sir Denby would just have said that Sir Francis used his key," Holmes said softly. "I very much doubt that the other murders could have been avoided. As it was, I was wavering between both men as the possible culprit. It was not until yesterday that my suspicions of Sir Denby were confirmed, and then only because he had access to the murder weapons that Sir Francis did not have."

"Weapons? Plural? What did he use?" Inspector Crawford sounded confused, and I admit that I felt much the same.

Holmes gestured at the polished cabinets. "Sir Denby used one, or more, of his prehistoric hand tools. They are heavy and hard, and the rounded end was perfect for applying a crushing blow to the skull."

I frowned. "But, Holmes, I have handled one of those tools. They are made of flint and the edges are still sharp, despite their great age. Surely Sir Denby would have cut his hand if he had grasped the blade in such a fashion?"

"If he had held it in his bare hand, then yes."

"He did not?" I was completely bewildered.

"On our first visit to the manor, I drew your attention to the suit of armour with the scratched gauntlet."

"He wore the gauntlet," I said, realization dawning. "The flint blade scratched the metal, but left his hand untouched. My God, Holmes! What a fiendish idea!"

"Indeed. The small flake of flint that I found in Miss Browning's hair was not from the surrounding ground, but had come off of the murder weapon."

One of the footmen tapped at the door to advise that several large, burly, policemen had arrived from Devizes, accompanying a closed coach from the Wiltshire County Lunatic Asylum. A sergeant, who was shown in to the room, informed Inspector Crawford that the chief constable himself, Captain Robert Sterne, R.N., had issued orders for Sir Denby to be housed at the asylum rather than at the police headquarters in Devizes. "For the safety of everyone, he said, Inspector."

"We shall take the news to the Leadbetters," Holmes said softly to Inspector Crawford. The inspector nodded his acknowledgement before hastening to join his colleagues.

We watched as the sedated form of Sir Denby was loaded into the coach by two heavy-set attendants from the asylum. Two police officers carrying Webley revolvers took positions on the footplate of the coach and beside the driver. The other police officers, including the sergeant, followed in a pony and trap. Inspector Crawford led the way in his own pony and trap. The sad little procession was watched in silence as it headed down the long drive from the manor and out onto the road to Devizes, leaving misery and devastation in its wake.

Chapter Twenty One

Holmes and I walked back down, for the last time, to the village. Mr. Wright was waiting for us with barely concealed curiosity. Everyone in the village had seen the closed carriage and knew what it meant.

"The killer's been caught, then, Mr. Holmes?"

"He has, Mr. Wright."

"Sir Francis?"

Holmes shook his head wearily. "Sir Denby." He ignored Mr. Wright's squawk of horror. "Could your lad Paul take us to the Leadbetters' place?"

"Of course, Mr. Holmes. Sir Denby. Who would've thought it?" Muttering to himself, and shaking his head in disbelief, Mr. Wright went to fetch his son.

"Who would have thought it, indeed," Holmes said with a sigh. "Well, we have certainly solved the mystery of Peter Harrington's death, though the cost is too high."

"The killer has been stopped," I reminded him.

"At the cost of four, possibly five more, lives. I should have caught him sooner," Holmes castigated himself. "I should have seen through the false bonhomie."

"But was it false, Holmes?" I asked softly. "Sir Denby was kind to his servants. He was obviously much loved by them. We know so little about the effects of melancholy and deep anguish upon the mind. Many lunatics are not madcaps, showing an eccentric face to the world. Not every lunatic is one who froths at the mouth or howls at the moon. The likes of the Illustrated Police News and the Penny Dreadfuls quite often get insanity horribly wrong."

"You comfort me, Watson. Though I am not sure that I deserve it. I have made a thorough hash of things."

I hated these dark moods that Holmes got into. "You found the murderer. That will be some comfort to those bereaved, such as Reverend Browning and his wife." I stopped speaking as Mr. Wright came back to tell us Paul was waiting out the front.

We walked out to the trap and sat in silence on the drive to the Leadbetters' farm.

Algernon Leadbetter took note of my friend's sombre mood when he came to the door. "You have news?" he asked softly.

"The murderer has been caught," I said, seeing that Holmes was not yet inclined to speak.

Algernon Leadbetter ushered us into the parlour, where his sister sat stitching at a small embroidery frame. Miss Leadbetter placed it to one side as we came in. She gave us an enquiring look. "Inspector Crawford is not with you?"

"I am afraid not, Miss Leadbetter," Holmes replied. "He had to return to Devizes."

I noted that Holmes did not say why.

Verity Leadbetter seemed slightly disappointed that Inspector Crawford was not with us. Tea was offered and declined. Algernon and Verity Leadbetter sat almost on the edge of their seats waiting for my friend to speak.

Holmes was silent for a long moment. He sighed. "You will soon hear the news. There is no pleasant way to put it. Sir Denby is the killer. He was caught after killing his wife and attempting to kill Sir Francis."

Both Leadbetters gave forth exclamations of shock.

"For Heaven's sake, Mr. Holmes, why?" cried Algernon.

"I doubt we will get a coherent reasons from Sir Denby. But I suspect it all stems from Lady Augusta's adultery with Sir Francis."

"Lady Augusta?" Algernon Leadbetter gaped at Holmes.

"The marriage was less than happy," my friend said softly. "I believe Sir Denby entertained the idea that he would be happier with a local women who shared his love of Wiltshire's prehistory."

"Who?" Miss Leadbetter asked.

"You," Holmes replied.

"What?" Verity Leadbetter looked shocked. Her brother was equally astounded. They stared at Holmes with expressions of mutual incomprehension.

"He was content for it to remain a mere fancy, until you privately announced your engagement to Peter Harrington, Miss Leadbetter. I believe that it was at that point Sir Denby realized that unless he did something it would simply remain a fancy. That is when he began to plot murder. But to remove Harrington was not enough, his wife would have to go too."

"Could he not have divorced Lady Augusta?" I asked doubtfully.

"Divorce is both expensive and rare, Watson," Holmes replied. "Then there is the stigma of being divorced. Whilst most of that clings to the woman, it can tarnish the man as well, making it unlikely that Mr. Leadbetter would have accepted Sir Denby marrying his sister."

Algernon Leadbetter nodded. "You are correct, Mr. Holmes. I would not have allowed a marriage to occur."

"Sir Denby is not the first man to view murder as a way to remove an unwanted spouse," said Holmes.

"But why kill Hyacinth Browning, and the others?" I asked.

Holmes was silent for a moment. "Sir Denby," he said slowly, "... for all his preference for prehistory, is something of a classicist. The contents of the manor's library clearly showed that. The Roman orator Marcus Tullius Cicero, in his speech 'Pro Roscio Amerino', asked the question: 'cui bono' – who profits? In this instance it would be clear who would profit from the deaths of Peter Harrington and Lady Augusta, but throw in several more deaths, all connected by the spurious threads of mythological tales and ornamented with swans' feathers, and the situation becomes a great deal more murky."

"My God!" Algernon Leadbetter exclaimed. "That is both ingenious and horrific." He paused for a moment, clearly thinking through the implications.

A troubled look came over his face. "Mr. Holmes. Does anyone else know about this?"

Holmes gave a tight, humourless, smile. "No, Mr. Leadbetter. Pray do not concern yourself. All the law is interested in is how the killings were done. Not why. I see no reason to give my thoughts on the case to the Wiltshire Constabulary and further endanger your sister's prospects."

Leadbetter let out a sigh of relief; his sister dropped her eyes to her lap, a slight flush burning her cheeks. I felt for her. Having been made sport of by Sir Francis, and her fiancé murdered, Verity Leadbetter's remaining prospects of marriage were grim enough, without the added burden of being at the centre of what was sure to be a sensational murder case.

"In truth," Holmes said softly, as if reading my thoughts, "I very much doubt that Sir Denby will go to trial. At the very end, he went to pieces. I think he will remain confined within the lunatic asylum, most likely for the rest of his life."

Knowing I was a doctor, Algernon Leadbetter looked at me for confirmation.

"I believe Holmes is right," I said, after a moment's reflection. "Once Sir Denby had killed his wife, he broke down. Something certainly caused his mind to snap. Certainly no sane man attempts to commit murder as publicly as he did with Sir Francis. Maybe he realized the enormity of what he had done. I do not know. He had to be heavily sedated with laudanum, after collapsing at the feet of his former nanny, clutching her skirts and weeping hysterically. I very much doubt that we will ever know the truth of the matter. And I very much doubt Sir Denby will be considered fit to plead in a court of law."

"The poor man," Verity whispered.

"Save your compassion for his children," Holmes advised gently. "Three youngsters left without parents. And for Reverend Browning and his wife who have lost their only child.

They deserve your pity and your charity much more than Sir Denby ever will."

Holmes tone grew hard. "Sir Denby took the first step towards his own destruction when he chose the path of a murderer. That he lost his sanity along the way is indeed a tragedy, but he did not need to take that path. No man ever needs to take the path of Cain. There is always another way. If one searches hard enough."

I noted that Holmes did not mention the estate workers and servants who would no doubt now be homeless. It was clear to me that he thought they had brought the situation upon themselves by endeavouring to conceal Sir Denby's crimes. I had to admit, that I felt similarly.

We left the Leadbetters and returned to Barrow-upon-Kennet in silence. Once back in our rooms, Holmes shook himself out of his dark mood long enough to say "Well, Watson, we have done all we can. What say we return to London?"

"It will have to be tomorrow," I said, consulting my pocket watch. "I very much doubt we will get a train from Marlborough to Swindon now. And if we did we would probably have to stay in Swindon overnight."

"True," Holmes agreed. "Best to leave it until the morning. The beds here are at least comfortable and the food is good. Which we cannot count upon in a railway hotel in Swindon."

The next morning saw us rise early and, having settled our bills, Paul drove us into Marlborough in the pub's pony and trap.

We had seated ourselves comfortably in a first class carriage, when we heard a shout from the platform. Looking out the window, we spotted Inspector Crawford coming along the platform obviously in search of us.

Holmes raised the window and leaned out. "Good morning, inspector."

"Ah there you are!" Inspector Crawford smiled to see us. "Good morning, Mr. Holmes, Doctor Watson. I just missed you at the pub."

"You came to wish us farewell?" I asked.

"I did, doctor, and also to let you know that Sir Francis is still in the land of the living, but the doctors are not sure if he will continue to be so. They said something about swelling of the brain. I also wished to ask how you got on with the Leadbetters. How did they take the news?"

"Both were somewhat taken aback to learn Sir Denby was the killer," I replied.

"And Miss Leadbetter, was she much distressed?" Inspector Crawford's almost careless tone did not fool me, let alone Holmes, who gave the inspector a wry smile.

"Miss Leadbetter is a compassionate young woman. She was naturally saddened to learn of Sir Denby's crimes." Holmes looked at Inspector Crawford, his eyes twinkling faintly. "I suggest you give it three months, inspector."

"Three months, Mr. Holmes?" Crawford's brow crinkled slightly as he tried to interpret Holmes' cryptic comment.

"Before you call upon the young lady." The twinkle in Holmes' eyes was obvious now. "Give it time for the scandal to subside somewhat," Holmes advised. "She will also be out of mourning for Harrington by then. I think you will find her amenable to your attentions."

The train whistled sounded, signalling that it was ready to depart. Inspector Crawford stammered his thanks, his cheeks suffused with colour, then stood back as there was a last minute rush of passengers for the train.

I sat back in my seat and watched the figure of the inspector recede as we pulled slowly out of Marlborough station

"Playing match-maker, Holmes?" I asked my friend with some amusement.

Holmes settled back into his seat and yawned gently. "Crawford is the sort of steady man that would be good for Miss Leadbetter." He snorted his amusement at my expression. "Come, Watson, you saw how he looked at her when we first visited the Leadbetters."

I thought back to that visit, and the gentle concern that the inspector had shown to the young woman. I realized that my friend was right. Inspector James Crawford would make an excellent husband for Miss Verity Leadbetter, if only Algernon Leadbetter agreed. I said as much to Holmes, who simply shook his head.

"Of course he will agree, Watson," Holmes said, leaning forward slightly. "James Crawford has a good position with the

Wiltshire Constabulary and is bound to go higher in the force. And if you are going to point out that he is a coachman's son, I would remind you that Harrington, though a lawyer, was the son of a butcher."

"True," I agreed, "And the Leadbetters themselves are a farming family."

Holmes nodded to acknowledge my point. "Now if you have no further comments to make, I shall take a nap. Kindly wake me when we arrive at Swindon."

With that Holmes settled back on his seat and shut his eyes, leaving me to gaze out of the window at the calm, green, beauty of the Wiltshire countryside. I resolved to ask Holmes to clear up a few niggling questions I had later, as he was clearly not in the mood to talk now.

Chapter Twenty Two

Once back in London, we became busy with further cases, and my questions slipped away as the events in Wiltshire receded in my memory. We became enmeshed in the case I have referred to in my writings as "The Five Orange Pips," with the tragic death of John Openshaw, and all thoughts of the Wiltshire case disappeared.

It was not until early October that the case was brought back to mind by the arrival in our rooms of Inspector James Crawford.

The pale afternoon sunshine was fighting to hold back the chill of autumn when Mrs. Hudson showed Inspector Crawford into our rooms. He took a seat beside the fire gratefully.

"What brings you to London, inspector?" I asked, as Crawford took a sip of the tea that Mrs. Hudson thoughtfully provided him.

"Two things, Doctor Watson."

"And they are?" Holmes asked from where he sat on the other side of the fireplace, nursing his own cup of tea and a plate of buttered crumpets.

"Firstly, to inform you that Miss Leadbetter has accepted my proposal of marriage. We shall be married next spring. We would be obliged if you gentlemen could attend."

We gave him our congratulations but did not commit to attending the wedding. Inspector Crawford did not push us on the subject.

"And the other reason?" I enquired.

Crawford sighed, and put his cup down on the table beside the chair. "Sir Denby," he said, his tone sad.

"The case has come to court?" I asked in surprise. To be honest, I had expected both Holmes and I to be called back to Wiltshire to testify before the court.

"No, Doctor Watson, and now it never will." He took a deep breath; he seemed to be steeling himself. "Sir Denby hanged himself two days ago."

"What?" I gaped at him.

"The authorities at the asylum kept him more or less permanently sedated. Or, at least, drugged enough that he was docile enough for them not to have to restrain him. Possibly the head of the asylum felt it was not quite the done thing to chain up a gentleman." Crawford's tone was sour.

"What happened?" Holmes demanded.

"Sir Denby made a noose from one of his bed sheets and tied it to the post of his bedstead. I am sure you can imagine the rest." The look on Inspector Crawford's face told me that he did not have to imagine it. No doubt he had been sent for when Sir Denby's body had been discovered.

"Those poor children are truly orphans now," I observed. "What will happen to them? And to the estate?"

"The oldest of Sir Denby's sisters and her husband have moved into Barrow Hill Manor," Crawford replied. "Their children are grown up. They are running the estate until young

Sir Henry is of age. Augustus will be joining his brother at boarding school shortly, and Elspeth will be going to live with another of Sir Denby's sisters, who has a daughter the same age. It was felt that it would be too hard for the children to remain in the place where their mother was murdered by their father."

"So Nanny McDonald has left?"

Crawford chuckled. "She is going with Elspeth. The sister has younger children still who could use a good nanny. Featherstone is retiring. He is broken by all this. David has stepped up to the position of butler, so there is still a Featherstone butlering at Barrow Hill Manor. Well, I must be going, gentlemen. I wish to get some small gift for Verity before I return home."

"One thing, inspector, Sir Francis Cigne, does he live?" I asked.

"Yes, Doctor Watson. He is a testament to your medical skills." Crawford gave me a small smile. "But he is a much changed man," he continued. "Sir Francis has returned to Melksham where his mother is nursing his physical injuries. I am told he is much subdued in character now, and has acquiesced to his mother finding a suitable wife for him. He will always walk with a limp as his ankle was shattered beyond full repair. If there is nothing else?"

I shook my head.

Inspector Crawford got to his feet. I stood up and showed him to the street door. I watched him stride down Baker Street, adroitly dodging the traffic. When I returned upstairs, Holmes was at the window watching the inspector wind his way along the street.

I sank back into my chair, my expression thoughtful. "You know, Holmes, there are a few things about the Wiltshire case that I never did ask you about. The inspector's visit has brought them back to mind."

Holmes returned to his chair. "Ask away, dear fellow." He reached for the Persian slipper containing his tobacco, and his pipe.

"I know why Peter Harrington and Lady Augusta were killed, and why Sir Denby attempted to kill Sir Francis, but why the others? Why kill Hyacinth Browning, Celeste Feuer, and Tobermoray Flyte. And why did he chose to stage their deaths as he did? I freely admit that I can see neither rhyme nor reason for those killings, as the saying goes."

"Let us take one at a time, shall we?" said Holmes. "As I said before, the rock placed on top of Harrington's corpse gave Sir Denby the idea to create his vicious dioramas, the victim's names helped him chose his myths."

"I do not understand."

"By unhappy mischance the name Peter means stone in Greek. Hyacinth Browning's situation was a direct copy from the myth of Apollo, Boreas and Hyacinthus, as Reverend Browning explained."

"But Mrs. Feuer's death? And Tobermoray Flyte's?"

"Mrs. Feuer's was Semele. I related that myth to you."

"And the lady turned out to be with child by Sir Francis." I was puzzled. "But how did Sir Denby know that, Holmes? The lady had not yet begun to show."

Holmes leaned back in his seat, his expression thoughtful. "I suspect, my dear Watson, that what occurred was that Sir Denby came across a distressed Celeste Feuer and coaxed the tale from her. Perhaps she thought Sir Denby could force Sir Francis to marry her. What it did was sign her death warrant." Holmes' expression hardened. "I have a little familiarity with the German language as you know."

I recalled our first case together where the word RACHE had been written on a wall in blood. A word that meant revenge in German, a fact that Holmes had pointed out to Lestrade and Gregson, much to their mutual chagrin.

"Your point being, Holmes?"

"Feuer, in German, means fire. While it would be interesting to discover how that word became a family name, the fact of the matter is that the name, combined with the lady's unfortunate situation, lead to the dreadful scene we witnessed."

"And Tobermoray Flyte?"

"That one, Watson, speaks for itself. I am sure you do not need me to point it out for you."

"Humour me," I suggested.

"The name Flyte and the manner of death of Icarus's death. Falling to his death whilst flying."

"Lady Augusta and Sir Francis?"

"In one of the myths, Jupiter came to the Spartan queen Leda in the guise of a swan, hence that dreadful tableaux."

I shuddered as I recalled that awful scene.

Holmes continued, "For Sir Francis, the myth used was that of Ixion. Ixion was a man much loved by Jupiter who invited him to dine with the gods upon Olympus. Ixion was the less than perfect house guest. The man attempted to outrage

Jupiter's wife Juno. For his presumption he was condemned to roll through the underworld strapped to a flaming wheel."

I stared at Holmes. "The scorch marks on the edge of the wheel that Inspector Crawford noticed. And the flare of a match that I noticed."

"Indeed. Things may well have gone much worse for Sir Francis if Sir Denby had succeeded in setting fire to the wheel."

I nodded, thinking back to Inspector Crawford's comments at Sir Francis' bedside that morning.

"I still do not understand where the wheel came from."

Holmes waved a hand dismissively. "No doubt it came from somewhere in one of the outbuildings upon the estate. Sir Denby most likely hid it inside the Prince's Barrow. He probably stored the wheel there not long after we visited it. You remember that Sir Denby commented that he would tell Nanny McDonald not to take the children up there for a while?"

"Ostensibly out of respect for the late Peter Harrington." I shook my head. "It was a dreadful case, Holmes. To be honest, I still do not understand why Sir Denby killed anyone except Harrington, Lady Augusta, and Sir Francis. Nor do I understand the motif of the swan's feathers."

"In the medieval period swans represented hypocrisy. Their white feathers were thought to conceal black skin. Sir Denby viewed Lady Augusta's coterie as hypocrites."

"But why, Holmes?"

"The Society of Ancient Virtues, my dear Watson. These virtues include gravitas and dignitas, as you noted when we arrived in Wiltshire. But the Romans had other virtues as well, including fidelis or faithfulness, and pudicitia or virtue.

Lady Augusta was not faithful to her marriage vows. Neither were Hyacinth Browning, or Celeste Feuer particularly virtuous. Sir Francis, with his predations, made a mockery of both faithfulness and virtue. As for Tobermoray Flyte…"

"I take your point," I said. "But what of Peter Harrington?"

"There you have me, Watson. We know little of the type of man Harrington was. But I suspect that he may have been intriguing with Lady Augusta as well."

"What?"

"I believe the note sent to him was possibly taken from Sir Francis Cigne's room by Sir Denby and used to lure Peter Harrington to the barrow. However, one must ask oneself why a man would go to such a meeting place on the basis of an unsigned note. The only reason can be that he recognized the handwriting. I am sure you can draw your own conclusions."

I could, and sighed deeply.

"As for the note itself," continued Holmes, "…you remember that I remarked upon the unevenness of the paper, where it had been cut with small bladed scissors?"

"I remember."

"Lady Augusta did that herself. To remove the Hardcastle family crest from the paper. In order to prevent anyone from recognizing the origin of the note."

"What about the other note? The one Lady Augusta sent you?"

Holmes sighed. "I misjudged badly, Watson," he admitted. "I thought Lady Augusta would send for my aid via one of the house staff. It did not occur to me that she would ask someone whose first instinct was to obey Sir Denby, not her."

A thought struck me. "Holmes, I can understand the myth of Ixion, but why Leda and the swan?"

Holmes gave a wintry chuckle. "Surely it is obvious, Watson."

"Not to me, Holmes."

"In French the word for swan is Cygne. It is spelled with a 'y' instead of an 'i', but it is pronounced the same way."

I stared at Holmes in shock.

Holmes was silent for a moment. "Would you do me a favour, Watson?"

"Of course, Holmes."

"I would rather you did not write of this case. But if you do, I ask that you please do not allow it to see the light of day until everyone involved is long dead."

Quietly, I gave him my assurances.

Holmes got to his feet, reaching for his violin. Then he stood, looking out into the gathering dusk and began to play.

I gazed into the flames in the fireplace in a melancholy mood as the soft strains of Tchaikovsky's "Swan Lake" drifted around the room.

AUTHOR'S NOTES

I could not resist setting my second book in Wiltshire, which is quite possibly my favourite English county.

Barrow Hill Manor and the village of Barrow-upon-Kennet do not exist except in my imagination and in this book. I imagined them as sitting about half way between Marlborough and Devizes. If the times getting between the village or manor and Devizes seem off, I ask your forgiveness. I could not find out how long it would take to make the journies in a pony and trap.

The Prince's Barrow is based upon West Kennet Long Barrow, a marvellous prehistoric tomb, whose excavation took place in the manner I mentioned. If you are ever in Wiltshire and get a chance to visit, I encourage you to do so. Silbury Hill is close by, so you get to see two wonderful prehistoric monuments at the same time.

I have John Watson express an interest in seeing Avebury, simply because I could not resist taking Holmes and Watson to Wiltshire and not at least mentioning Avebury. Visiting Avebury is an experience I would recommend to anyone with an interest in prehistory. Unlike Stonehenge you can get up close to the stones. The fact that an entire village is built inside the circles should give you an idea as to its size.

Hand axes were the Swiss army knives of prehistory. Mostly tear-drop shaped, they were knapped (chipped) from flint or chert and used for anything from cutting up meat, to skinning carcasses, to clearing scrub. I was privileged to be allowed to hold such an axe at the British Museum in London when I visited a couple of years ago. Just holding it gave me an incredible feeling of continuity with the past. To hold something made by a remote ancestor was a mind-blowing experience. The British Museum has several hands-on desks where you can handle various items. As a way to experience history, it cannot be beaten.

By the late 1800s the custom of serving special funeral biscuits and wine was beginning to fade away. I chose to use it in this book because I felt that in a small village, the older ritual would most likely still be in practice. If you are curious, you can find several recipes for funeral biscuits on the internet.

Two books proved to be invaluable when writing this one. "Keeping Their Place" by Pamela Sambrook, and "Life Below Stairs" by Sian Evans. Both books helped flesh out the servants of Barrow Hill Manor, and give a feel for country manor life in the late 19th century. I had wanted to include Dorothy Watts from my first book, but what I learned from these two books made me realize that I could not do so believably and have her keep her secret. That more than anything is the reason that this book is set two years before the first.

There were two other books that were almost as important. One was a recent edition of Bulfinch's "Age of Fable." It was slightly twee, and extremely Victorian, but ultimately helpful. But if you are curious to read about the myths of Ancient Greece, I suggest Stephen Fry's recent books "Mythos" and "Heroes." The style is much more readable.

The second book was "Wiltshire Folk Tales" by Kirsty Hartsiotis. This book gave me a feel for the area, not to mention inspiration to create my tale of the origins of the Wight and Barrel pub.

I have to thank Craig Janacek whose Holmes and Watson chronology helped me get my dates right. Craig, you don't know me from Adam, but your chronology was a life saver. Thank you. If anyone is interested, you can find the chronology at https://craigjanacek.wordpress.com/2015/09/13/a-chronological-order-of-sherlock-holmes-stories/

Many thanks to Dr. Andrea Williams Ph.D. for her knowledge of medieval symbolism, the French language, and her willingness to put up with weird texts from me at all hours. Thank you, my friend.

Thanks are also due to Steve Emecz at MX Publishing, who was prepared to take a punt on my first book. You made a life-long dream come true, thank you Steve.

Lightning Source UK Ltd.
Milton Keynes UK
UKHW021830091220
374886UK00005B/187